I0548394

The Poisoned Penman

Another Adventure of Enoch Hale with Sherlock Holmes

Dan Andriacco and Kieran McMullen

First edition published in 2014
© Copyright 2014
Dan Andriacco and Kieran McMullen

The right of Dan Andriacco and Kieran McMullen to be identified as the author of this work has been asserted by them in accordance with the Copyright, Designs and Patents Act 1998.

All rights reserved. No reproduction, copy or transmission of this publication may be made without express prior written permission. No paragraph of this publication may be reproduced, copied or transmitted except with express prior written permission or in accordance with the provisions of the Copyright Act 1956 (as amended). Any person who commits any unauthorised act in relation to this publication may be liable to criminal prosecution and civil claims for damage.

All characters appearing in this work are fictitious or used fictitiously. Except for certain historical personages, any resemblance to real persons, living or dead, is purely coincidental. The opinions expressed herein are those of the authors and not of MX Publishing.

Paperback ISBN 978-1-78092-633-9
ePub ISBN 978-1-78092-634-6
PDF ISBN 978-1-78092-635-3

Published in the UK by MX Publishing
335 Princess Park Manor, Royal Drive,
London, N11 3GX
www.mxpublishing.co.uk
Cover design by www.staunch.com

Grateful acknowledgment to Conan Doyle Estate Ltd. for the use of the Sherlock Holmes characters created by Sir Arthur Conan Doyle.

Dan Andriacco dedicates this book to

NUNO ROBLES

Kieran McMullen dedicates this book to

CHARLES MALTESE

CONTENTS

ONE
Tea Time for Death

"It *began* with the tea," the Hatter replied.
– Lewis Carroll, *Alice's Adventures in
Wonderland*

"Good work again, Hale." Nigel Rathbone looked up from the typed pages in his hand and favored his employee with a rare smile. "Tomorrow this story will be a leader in newspapers from Manchester to Massachusetts."

Enoch Hale, a tall American with a narrow face and a pencil-thin mustache, had presented his boss with the third installment in a series of articles about rum running. The managing director of the Central Press Syndicate, the fourth largest press association in the world and coming on strong under Rathbone's reign, couldn't get enough of it.

"Thanks," Hale said, lighting a celebratory panatela, "but there's an even bigger story to bag. I'm hoping all this ink will bring forward some concrete leads on the British part of the operation. No other journalists have touched that yet."

"Hope doesn't sell newspapers, my lad." The sparkle in the South African's hazel eyes belied the rebuke in his words.

"Yes, sir. What I meant to say is, I'm working on it."

Hale was convinced that this would be the biggest story he'd worked on since coming to London, bigger even than the Hangman Murders[1], if he could nail it all down. Illegal booze had become a huge international business since the Volstead Act brought Prohibition to the States two and a half years before. Some of the stuff was home grown—bathtub gin and the like—but some high-quality alcohol was being shipped from England to please the more sophisticated palates and bigger pocketbooks of America. Hale had written a general outline of how that worked in his first three stories. Now came the hard part—nailing down the rumors and speculation that he'd come across in his research.

Sources on Wall Street, where Hale had worked before the Great War and still had family connections, had told him that Scotch was being moved out of England over the signature of a stockbroker named Joseph P. Kennedy. From there it was sent to the States on boats controlled by another Irish-American, William McCoy.

According to the sources, this McCoy had at his command a whole fleet of boats that moved alcohol to what was called "The Rum Line" three miles off shore of the U.S. There, fishermen and lobstermen would pick up loads and run them in to customers like "Big Bill" Dwyer, an Irish mobster in New York, by way of Northport and Greenport on the North Shore of Long Island. There were only two Coast Guard cutters on the North Shore, and Hale's informants told him that Dwyer paid off the cops and Coast Guard. Northport had an underground tunnel

---

[1] See *The Amateur Executioner*, MX Publishing Co., 2013.

system with speakeasies, storehouses, and a bowling alley, but the booze didn't stop there. It went into New York City on roads like the Vanderbilt Motor Parkway. The Vanderbilt, known as Rum Runner's Road, was a privately owned 48-mile concrete road open to the public for a toll. It had been built by the rich as a convenient way to get to their "bungalows" in the Hamptons. Since it was private property the cops couldn't patrol it.

All of that was on the American end of the scheme. Here in Britain, Hale had put out feelers over the past several weeks to try to identify suppliers, shippers, paid-off customs officials, dockworkers, and union bosses who were involved. Surely his three-part series would jog loose a memory or rouse a suspicion in someone willing to talk to an enterprising reporter.

"Don't expect the next piece by teatime," Hale told Rathbone, "but it'll be worth waiting for." *Someone is orchestrating all this from here, and I intend to find out who and how.*

"Tea, Hale?" Langdale Pike asked, looking up from a notebook in which he was writing. He was a small man, except for an outsized head decorated with gray mutton-chop whiskers. Lights in the chandelier above him danced off of his pink scalp.

"Of course. Earl Grey would be nice." Hale preferred coffee, but when in London . . .

That afternoon, Hale had presented himself upon request at Pike's club, Arthur's, after half a day spent on the London Docks in pursuit of a lead. Such variety in the course of his day had been a major reason that Hale, inspired by a fellow volunteer ambulance driver named Hemingway, had gone into this line of work after the war. The horror with which his Fleet Street profession filled his family back in Boston and New York was icing on the cake.

Hale's Brahmin roots and Brooks Brothers suit always stood him in good stead at Arthur's, however.

Established in 1811 as the first club formed by member ownership, Arthur's was one of the reasons the area around Pall Mall and St. James's Street had long been nicknamed "Clubland." While each club had its own quirks and particularities, they shared a propensity for tall ceilings, huge paintings, marble statues, and (except for the Reform Club) grand staircases in the entrance hall.

The building, at 69 St. James's Street, stood four stories high but was divided into only two floors. Langdale Pike sat at a table right in front of one of the four large windows on the ground floor, next to the front entrance on the far right of the building. He'd sat there every day for more than twenty years, collecting and then reselling gossip in the form of paragraphs for the trash papers.

"I always drink Caribbean Black Sage myself," Pike said. "Good for my gout. It was recommended to me."

He stopped writing, closed the notebook, and stuck it in the breast pocket of his unstylish three-piece gray suit. Hale allowed himself the passing fancy that the small volume must contain a wonderful collection of secrets.

Pike hailed a passing waiter, a young man with longish blond hair, and asked him to bring Mr. Hale a cup of Earl Grey. Pike's own tea lay on the table in front of him. As soon as the waiter disappeared, he took a long sip.

"You said that you had some information I'd be interested in," Hale prodded, impatient with the civilities. "What's so special that you couldn't just tell me on the telephone?"

Ever since Hale's friend Tom Eliot had introduced him to Pike during that Hangman Murders business, he had occasionally contacted Pike for the sort of information that only Pike would have. Small amounts of Hale's personal funds had passed into Pike's hands in appreciation. But this time it was different; this time, Pike had come to him.

"I had to be careful speaking on the telephone, my good fellow." Pike looked around and then leaned forward, speaking in a low voice. "This isn't just cheap goss—"

Stopping in mid-word, he fell forward as if suddenly weak.

"Pike!" Hale moved quickly across the table and felt the older man's wrist. Pike's pulse was weak, his hand icy.

"Somebody call a doctor!" Hale yelled. The words were barely out of his mouth when he felt Pike's pulse stop beneath his fingers. The strange little man was dead.

Acting on an impulse that he could never explain even to himself, Hale reached into the breast pocket of Pike's coat. He transferred the notebook inside, the one that Hale fantasized as being full of secrets, into his own pocket before anyone else got near the body.

TWO
Coshed!

"I was following you, of course."
"Following me? I saw nobody."
    – "The Adventure of the Devil's Foot"

Rum running forgotten, Hale spent the rest of the day writing a story that was part first-person account of Pike's death and part obituary.

> Langdale Pike, a fixture in the front window of Arthur's Club for more than two decades, died there on Tuesday afternoon in the presence of this reporter after suffering an apparent heart attack. He was 64 years old.
> Mr. Pike, known to have a large circle of friends from all classes, made what was said to be a comfortable living writing paragraphs . . .

The story quoted Tom Eliot, Hale's banker friend who wrote poetry on the side, as lauding Pike's "amazing knowledge of the world even though he saw so little of it." The retired detective Sherlock Holmes said that Pike "had he chosen to turn his talents to the science of deduction would have been in the first rank of sleuths." Holmes, who Hale reached by telephone at his home on the Sussex Downs, had been a contributor to and, on certain occasions, a beneficiary of Pike's vast fund of social knowledge in the later years of his detective work.

Before leaving Arthur's, Hale had tried unsuccessfully to prod similar quotes from members that he found on the scene. But the likes of Colonel Clownes, Sir W. Farquhar-Bart, Lord Worsley, and George Standish, M.P., seemed embarrassed by the professional gossip in their midst and loathe to be associated with him in print. The penman's membership in the club was a sort of legacy—his father, the late Sir Blackford Pike, had been a member before him. Although the byline of Langdale Pikewas generally assumed to be a coy pseudonym drawn from a trio of scenic peaks known as the Langdale Pikes in Westmorland, it was in fact his real name.

"So the Pike family has devolved from knight to gossipmonger in a single generation," Rathbone mused in his clipped South African accent. "What you've written is fine, Hale, but I smell a second-day story there."

"Nobody seemed to really know much about Pike's personal life, not even Holmes." Hale suspected that the detective knew more than he was telling, but the reporter kept that to himself. "I did find out that he lived with his sister, a woman named Lydia Grayson. I'll try talking to her tomorrow."

But that was not to happen for several days.

As he was tidying up his desk for the night, Hale was surprised to look up and see Horace Harker still hovering around. Retired long ago, the old man with a bald head and a turkey-like beak of a nose haunted the offices of the Central Press Syndicate like the ghost of journalists past. He was a relic of the previous century, the late Victorian era, when reporters wrote their stories in long hand. That world was far removed from the news agency of today, with the *clickety-clack* sound of typewriters at work forming a constant background noise in the Fleet Street offices.

"I heard that my old friend Pike died today," he said. Harker, clad in shirtsleeves and braces stretched over his pot belly, must have been a generation older than the dead man.

"You heard right," Hale acknowledged. "I just wrote the story. First-person account."

"You were there when it happened, eh? Was he shot?"

"No, no, nothing like that," Hale said. "He just collapsed."

"Oh, poison then."

"What are you talking about? Pike died of a heart attack."

Harker guffawed. "Don't be silly, young man. He was murdered, of course. Men like Pike don't die in their beds. Did I ever tell you how in that business of the six Napoleons I—"

Frequently, Hale thought. He tuned out. Harker had a tendency to ramble on, somehow usually working in an inaccurate account of the one important story of his career. The notion that Pike had been murdered was nonsense, surely, the product of a wandering mind. The gossip-monger's unexpected death was a two-day story that would be wrapped up by an interview with the sister. Then Hale could get back to chasing down rumrunners.

After murmuring a few polite words to Harker, including an assurance that he would take up the old man's theory with Scotland Yard, Hale left the office. His flat on Claverton Street, near St. George Square, was a good three miles away. He walked down Fleet Street in the gathering gloom of the June evening toward the Strand, looking for a hack. He had gone but a short way when up ahead of him, at number 22 Fleet, he saw Ye Olde Cock Tavern. The venerable pub dated back to 1549 and had been at that location since 1887, according to Tom Eliot, his walking guidebook to London. Being of a literary bent, Eliot was fascinated with the men of letters who had hoisted pints there in their day—Samuel Pepys, Charles Dickens, Dr. Samuel Johnson . . .

Perhaps the name of Enoch Hale should be added to that list tonight. Not just a historical curiosity, Ye Olde Cock Tavern was still well known for its great cask ales and pub food. It would be a convenient place for Hale to quaff a drink or two and take a closer look at the notebook he had slipped out of Pike's coat. In the rush to get out the story, he'd only been able to glance at a few pages. He hadn't even told Rathbone about it because . . . well, he didn't know why. He'd just felt like keeping that information to himself.

Hale had just settled on this very appealing course of action when, from the darkened alleyway on the left leading to the Temple Church, he caught sight of a blurry figure out of the corner of his eye. He turned, but too late. A heavy blow descended on his head. The world dissolved into utter darkness.

THREE
Murder

"I've never killed anyone, but I frequently get satisfaction
reading the obituary notices."
  – Clarence Darrow, newspaper interview in
    Chicago

"Somehow my years of boxing and fencing at Yale,
as well as less genteel fisticuffs, didn't prove particularly
useful against a man with a cosh," Hale said ruefully. "I
didn't even know I was being followed until it was too late.
I'll never make that mistake again."

On the morning after the attack, the back of his
head was still pounding worse than any hangover he'd ever
had. Upon awakening in the alley last night, he'd
immediately gotten sick.

"It was a man, then?" asked Chief Inspector Henry
Wiggins, with a hint of amusement seldom seen in the hard-
driving police official.

"I certainly hope so!"

Feeling foolish, Hale had just finished explaining that he hadn't seen his assailant and couldn't provide even the sketchiest description.

Without any real hope that it would make a difference, Hale had presented himself to Wiggins at his New Scotland Yard office first thing in the morning to report the assault. Their paths had crossed often enough for Hale to consider the wiry, middle-aged copper a friend of sorts. Wiggins was a tough bird, raised on the streets. Hale, despite the disadvantage of wealth and privilege, had considered himself tough as well. Until last night.

"Can you give me a list of what was in the stolen wallet?"

"Sure. I'll write it out for you. There's nothing wrong with my memory."

Wiggins slid a sheet of paper over to Hale's side of the desk. The American wrote down:

Letter from Mother
Cash
Central Press Syndicate identification card
Photo of Sadie
Telephone Numbers—Key Sources

"Obviously, none of that has value to anyone but me, except for the money," Hale said.

"How much money?"

Hale shifted uneasily. "Fifty pounds, mostly in small bills."

"Fifty!" Wiggins's sandy eyebrows shot up. That was as much money as an honest chief inspector like him would earn in two months, Hale knew. Neither his CPS salary nor his expense account from the tight-fisted Syndicate accounted for the wad of bills in Hale's wallet. He still received a grudging allowance from his parents back in Boston.

"When I'm trying to get information, I've found that cash is a very good tongue-loosener," he said, somewhat defensively.

"You're lucky you didn't get killed down on the docks for that kind of money," Wiggins chided. His eyes continued through the list of items in the stolen wallet. "Still keeping company with Miss Briggs, I see. When are you going to make an honest woman out of her, Hale?"

The journalist thought of the photo, which scarcely did justice to Sadie's natural blond hair and flawless skin, and winced. Wiggins had no way of knowing that he was poking at an open wound.

Two years before, on the night of the first Hangman Murder, Hale had met and soon fallen in love with a music hall singer known as Sadie Briggs. Only later, after a comedy of errors, had he found out that she was really Lady Sarah Bridgewater, daughter of the fifth Earl of Sedgewood. The family was not only titled, but still wealthy. In the typical manner of British nobility, Edward Bridgewater had been outraged to find out that his daughter spent her evenings as a common music hall singer. Somewhat mollified by her use of a stage name, he had tolerated her inexplicable career while doing everything possible to discourage it.

Perhaps even worse, in Lord Sedgewood's view, was her romance with an American journalist. The idea of marriage, he had made quite clear to his daughter, was unthinkable. Sadie—as Hale still thought of her—had been unwilling to press the issue, lest her father use his influence to make sure she never appeared on stage again. Hale's pride kept him from informing the Earl that he was no penniless scribbler looking to marry into a fortune; he had money of his own and had walked away from even more. If that's what his Lordship thought of him . . .

None of that mattered right now anyway.

"Sadie's leaving the country for a while, actually," Hale said, trying to keep his voice casual. "She's going to Egypt with her father. I won't see her for some months after tonight."

"Oh. Sorry to hear that, Hale. She's quite a charming lass." Wiggins looked back at Hale's list of what had been in his wallet. "These telephone numbers you mention—that would be for people who give you information?"

"That's it. And you're in very good company, Chief Inspector."

"How flattering. So this list and the wallet itself are all that was taken?"

"That's all."

But Hale was lying. The ruffian had also removed Pike's notebook from his breast pocket. He couldn't tell Wiggins that without confessing to having taken it from Pike's body. Although not yet completely familiar with British law, Hale was reasonably sure that was at least a minor crime.

Wiggins looked thoughtful. "Well, I suppose that list of sources might be of interest to somebody."

Head still thumping, it took Hale longer than it should have to see the implications of the police official's musings. "You don't think this was just about money? Lord knows I had plenty of it on me."

"How would some garden variety thief know that? Of course, you do dress like a bit of a toff. But why cosh you like that? Our thieves generally aren't that violent in the better neighborhoods. And it was a bit of a risk, wasn't it? Fleet Street isn't exactly deserted at that time of night. What really bothers me, though, is the coincidence that this attack and robbery should be carried out on the man who was present with Langdale Pike when he died."

"Why is that such a coincidence?"

"Because, Hale, Pike was murdered."

Enoch Hale was not the only person whom Chief Inspector Henry Wiggins informed about the coroner's findings. Some hours before Hale went to New Scotland Yard, and some miles away on the Sussex Downs, a beekeeper hung up his telephone and brooded.

Sherlock Holmes had never completely reconciled himself to the instrument. Only at the insistence of his housekeeper, Martha, had he installed one in his villa by the sea when he retired from active practice as a consulting detective.

Retirement had proved elusive and illusory, however. After almost twenty years on the Downs, he kept being pulled back—back to London, back to the world of crime and detection. It couldn't be helped, he thought with a sigh. When he had read Hale's account of Pike's death, he had been as certain as he ever had of anything that it was murder. And his old friend Wiggins had just confirmed his suspicions with a telephone call.

He pulled out his Bradshaw to see when the next train left for London.

FOUR
Lovers Parting

Men always want to be a woman's first love—women like
to be a man's last romance.
> – Oscar Wilde, *A Woman of No Importance*

The woman known to thousands of music hall
enthusiasts—and to herself, much of the time—as Sadie
Briggs looked at her handsome beau with astonishment.

"Poison!" she exclaimed, her green eyes even wider
than usual. She immediately regretted it, knowing that she
sounded like a girl. And here she was almost twenty-three
and claimed to be two years older. But Enoch didn't seem
to notice. He just nodded.

"Pike's tea was laced with prussic acid, a very fast-
acting poison," he said, "and I watched him drink it.
Wiggins says the stuff tastes like bitter almonds, but would
have been masked by the strong flavor of Pike's beloved
Caribbean Black Sage Tea."

"So Scotland Yard found the poison in the tea?"

"Not there—the tea was thrown out before
Scotland Yard got interested. But the body showed signs of
prussic acid. It seems that even after death the body will

bloat slightly and rather quickly and the blood turns a cherry red and stays that way for quite a while. There is some slight foam in the mouth also."

"Only the finest, refined dinner conversation here! Ugh!" Sadie shivered theatrically. "Well, poison is easy to trace, isn't it? Don't people have to sign for it at the chemist's?" She had read something of the sort in a mystery by that woman Agatha Christie.

"Only if that's where you get it. Prussic acid is made in huge quantities for the mining industry, and it's also used in gold plating, engraving, explosives, and in rat and insect poison. An industrious sort can even make it from crushed apple seeds, apricot pits, cherry pits, and bitter almonds. People can actually kill themselves by eating too many bitter almonds."

"I'll keep that in mind, Enoch. Should it worry me that you know so much about poison?"

"I didn't until Wiggins instructed me this morning. The interesting question is why Wiggins was looking for poison to begin with."

Sadie leaned forward. "And why was that?"

"I don't know for sure—because Wiggins refused to tell me," Enoch said, with the air of a man delivering a punch line. "But I think it had something to do with Sherlock Holmes. He and Pike did each other favors for years. Holmes is supposed to be retired with his bees, but we know from experience that's something of an exaggeration.

"Anyway, you can read my story in tomorrow's papers—such as it is. I mostly just quoted Wiggins because that's all I have. I went to Pike's house to try to get some comments from his sister, but she wasn't home."

Enoch stopped talking as a waiter set down a slab of beef and started carving. What a strange discussion this was to be having over dinner at Simpson's, especially their farewell dinner. But that was life around Enoch Hale—you never knew what he would be doing or talking about next. Oh, how she would miss him over these next several months!

Sadie wore a simple but fashionable headband, a string of pearls, and a navy blue French couture dress that she had bought on a recent shopping trip to Paris. Her father had insisted she take the quick trip to Paris before they departed for months in the desert. It had either been very kind of him or just another way to try to keep her away from "that American." In either case, it had been fun.

When the waiter left, she said, "Do you think the waiter did it?"

Enoch jabbed his thumb in the direction of their departing server. "Him?"

"No, silly, the waiter at Pike's club."

"Highly unlikely, I should think. Wiggins interviewed him, of course, and said he'd acted like a scared rabbit. Who wouldn't, being questioned by Scotland Yard about a murder that happened right under your nose? And I saw the fellow myself—he's just a lad. What reason would he have for killing Pike?"

"What reason could anybody have? Oh, I know! It was all those embarrassing things he wrote about people."

"That's what Wiggins thinks."

"And what do you think, Enoch?"

He reached across the table and took Sadie's hand. She felt a tingle and a warm glow as she studied his handsome face, dashing mustache, and light brown hair combed straight back. "I think, my poppet, that we have other things to talk about. You are about to desert me for some musty old mummies and I'm damned cross about it."

Enoch had never appreciated the romance of Egyptology. Sadie had to admit to herself—but not to him—that her father had gone a bit round the bend on the subject. But it wasn't just about the tombs for him. Daddy was in a competition with his life-long rival, Lord

Carnarvon, to make a major find in the Valley of the Kings. Rumor was that Carnarvon's man Howard Carter was getting close. Daddy had decided he must go to Egypt himself to negotiate in person the rights for the leader of his own expedition, Linwood Baines, to excavate in some choice spots in the Valley of the Kings. At Daddy's urging, she had reluctantly agreed to go along.

"Oh, Enoch, I'm not deserting you. You know that."

"I suppose so," he admitted. "I also know that your father just wants to get you away from the music hall and away from me, in no particular order."

She gently stroked his slender fingers. "It's only for a few months. That really can't make such a difference in the long run, can it? Daddy has really been such a dear about my singing, after he got over the initial shock. It will make him so happy if I do this."

"Right." Something about the emphasis in the way he said it make Enoch sound like a Brit, Sadie thought with amusement. "I'm sure it will make that stuffed shirt Alfie Barrington happy, too."

He looked so serious that she couldn't help laughing. "Good heavens, you're jealous because Alfie's going with us! That's so silly. Alfie and I grew up together. He's been like a second son to Daddy ever since Charles took off."

Alfred Barrington, second son of the Duke of Somerset, was nothing at all like Enoch Hale—not as tall, not as handsome, and not as amusing.

"Ah, yes, your wastrel brother, Charles. I've been intrigued by the fellow ever since you told me your father disinherited him over his dissolute ways. He sounds like a scoundrel after my own heart. I even asked Pike to see if he could find out what happened to him after he disappeared."

"You what!" Sadie felt an unexpected flash of anger. Damn Enoch. His journalistic nosiness could spoil everything. And besides, he didn't understand. The War had changed Charles. It wasn't his fault, really.

Enoch looked shocked at her reaction, but recovered quickly. "Well, no matter now, my dear," he said lightly, "poor Pike is dead."

Still, Sadie wondered whether that would be the end of it.

"I'll miss you, sugar," Hale went on.

She touched his face. "Come now, don't look like such a sad hound dog. You'll be so busy with your rumrunners and murderers and the like that the time will pass quickly. You'll hardly notice I'm gone."

"Fat chance of that," her beau said gloomily.

"Well, we still have tonight."

FIVE
Notes from the Dead

Death keeps no calendar.
  – George Herbert, *Outlandish Proverbs*

Hale felt badly that he hadn't been entirely forthcoming with Sadie on their last evening together before she left England, but he had left some things unsaid for her own peace of mind.

Since early in their relationship, Sadie had always been unreasonably fearful for his safety. That's why he hadn't told her about being coshed. He also hadn't shared with her two possible motives for Pike's murder—to stop him from telling Hale whatever he'd planned to tell him over tea, or to conceal whatever Pike had written in the notebook that someone had taken a great risk to steal from Hale.

He'd informed Rathbone about the notebook immediately upon returning from Scotland Yard that morning.

"And you're just now telling me this?" The South African had sounded like an angry father who was not only displeased but disappointed.

"I'm sorry, sir." Hale had tried to sound contrite. He'd always hated parental confrontations, of which he'd had many. "It didn't seem that important until someone stole it and I found out that Pike had been murdered. Besides, I didn't know how you'd react. I mean, you've never told me to steal anything." *Not in so many words.*

Rathbone's energy and determination to get the news had brought new life to a once-moribund news syndicate. He roamed the office and snapped out orders like a cowboy cracking a whip, without a trace of English reserve. But, then, he wasn't English.

He had seen promise in Hale and lured him away from *The Evening Journal,* where Hale had first landed a job after his volunteer service in Italy during the war. A few weeks ago he had managed to hire the legendary Ned Malone away from *The Daily Gazette.* Malone had first gained fame a decade earlier when he'd reported the incredible story of the Challenger-Roxton expedition to the Lost World, in which he had taken no small part. Malone had been first with many important stories since, several of them involving his good friend Professor Challenger.

For all these reasons, Hale deeply respected his boss and craved his approval.

"React?" Rathbone repeated. "I applaud your initiative, of course! I would have done the same thing—if I'd been there and if I'd thought of it." Quickly slipping into a mellower mood, Rathbone lit a curved pipe. "It's just unfortunate that we shan't benefit from the fruits of your enterprise."

Hale smiled. "That's not entirely true." He explained that he had paged briefly through the notebook before settling down to write his initial story about the death of Langdale Pike. He recalled seeing a few names.

"That's not much to go on," Hale admitted, "but it's a start."

"Excellent!" Rathbone's voice crackled with the excitement of a hound on the scent. Hale could almost imagine the editor's long, sharp nose twitching. "Until further notice, Hale, you're on this story full-time."

"But the rumrunners—"

"—can wait," Rathbone said firmly. "They aren't going to disappear as long as the Americans continue with their Prohibition nonsense."

So after writing his story, and before dinner with Sadie, Hale had begun running down leads. On Thursday morning, struggling with feelings of sadness and a slight hangover in the wake of his departure from Sadie the night before, he gave Rathbone a status report. It had been two days since the murder.

"Pike's sister wasn't home. I'll try again later. Now that we know it's a matter of murder, I'm even more eager to talk to her about her brother."

Rathbone nodded agreement. "And the notebook?" he prodded. "You were going to follow up on what you remembered of it."

"Right. It was a small leather-bound volume that fit easily into his—and my—breast pocket. The pages on the right were an appointment diary. Those on the left were for general notes. I remembered seeing appointments in recent days with Harrison Scott, George Standish, and G.K.C.— presumably the great Chesterton himself. My own name was there, too, in the freshest ink. One of the notes said something about S.H. Benson's. I haven't talked to any of them yet, but I spent a bit of time yesterday finding out who they all are."

Rathbone chuckled. "Well, there's certainly no mystery about Chesterton. Has the man ever had an unwritten thought? Or an uninteresting one?"

Gilbert Keith Chesterton was one of the most extraordinary men of that or any other day—mystery writer, poet, essayist, journalist, theologian, economic thinker, and artist. His written output was enormous. To some, he was best known as the creator of the humble detective Father Brown. To others, he was the defender of traditional Christianity in his book *Orthodoxy* or the author of a weekly column in the *Illustrated London News*.

Chesterton cut a familiar figure wherever he went, with his great bandit's mustache, broad-brimmed hat, swordstick, and a cape draped over his huge frame. And he was often a controversial one as well. Two months ago he had finally gone too far, in the opinion of his old friend and antagonist, George Bernard Shaw, by being received into the Roman Catholic Church.

"Gossip writer meets eminent man of letters," Hale said. "It's hard to see how that could have anything to do with Pike's death, but I look forward to asking G.K.C. what he and Pike talked about. With Chesterton, it could have been anything."

"The great Gaels of Ireland
Are the men that God made mad,
For all their wars are merry,
And all their songs are sad."

This last came from Harker, standing in the doorway, looking more than ever like a superannuated turkey with his beak nose, wrinkled neck, and bald head.

"What's that?" Rathbone snapped. He would have fired Harker long ago, Hale was certain, if Harker weren't already retired. The managing director seemed to regard the old man as a part of the furniture, along with the bronze statue of Queen Victoria in the Syndicate's foyer that young reporters used to butt their cigarettes.

"Chesterton," Harker explained, with the air of one stating the perfectly obvious. "*The Ballad of the White Horse,* Book II, 'The Gathering of the Chiefs.'"

"God spare me the Irish," Hale muttered. He'd had enough of them in the Hangman business.

Harker heard him. "There's an old saying, Mr. Hale. 'God invented whiskey to keep the Irish from ruling the world.' I read your rumrunner stories—good work, for an American."

Hale began to wonder whether Harker wasn't himself overly familiar with the "water of life."

"Get out of my office, Harker," Rathbone demanded. "If you do not leave immediately I shall have you removed from the premises by force with instructions that you are never to enter the building again. Do I make myself clear?"

Harker stood up straighter, sad-faced but as erect as a man of his age could be. "You do not have to shout, sir. My hearing is as keen as ever. I bid you good day." He turned and left.

"I haven't been able to find out a thing about Harrison Scott," Hale said, continuing as if there had been no interruption. "He isn't listed in any city directory or social directory. Maybe Standish can tell me something about him."

"Now *that* name has a familiar ring."

Hale nodded. "It should. George Standish, O.B.E., is quite a wealthy fellow with interests in shipping from here to Cuba. He's also a rising Member of Parliament, expected to become President of the Board of Trade if the Tories gain power in October. My friend Willie Gordon, who covers politics for *The Morning Star*, says that a lot of people think he could become Prime Minister someday."

"A lot of people have been thinking that about Winston Churchill for years. 'Some day' hasn't come yet."

"Yes, sir. I also found out that Standish is chairman of the management committee of Arthur's. I expect that puts him in a rather tricky position at times. Arthur's is a purely social club—no politics allowed."

"That just leaves S.H. Benson," Rathbone said. "Who's he?"

"Samuel Herbert Benson. But the entry that I remember seeing said 'S.H.Benson's,' with an apostrophe. That's a big ad agency that Benson started and named after himself in 1893. His son's been running it for the past eight years."

"So something about this Benson's agency must have attracted Pike's attention."

"That's what it looks like."

Rathbone sat back, puffing on his pipe. "The chances that what you happen to remember from Pike's notebook have anything to do with his murder are rather slim, don't you think? In fact, for all we know, there may not even be anything incriminating in the entire notebook. The murderer probably went after it based on what he *assumed* was in it. Still, you have an angle. What are you waiting for? Get on it, Hale!"

SIX
Questions in Clubland

No place in England where everyone can go is
considered respectable. This is the genesis of the club.
— George Moore, *Confessions of a Young Man*

Within the half-hour, Hale was approaching the
marble steps of 69 St. James's Street for a return visit to
Arthur's. He was just in time to save a former colleague
from an embarrassing injury.

As Hale's foot touched the bottom marble step, he
heard a commotion above him. A slight male body came
stumbling backward out the front door, accompanied by
the sharp command, "And don't come back!"

Showing the presence of mind and body that had
helped him more than once during the Great War, as well as
in numerous bar fights at after-hours clubs, Hale put out his
arms. The man fell right into them.

"You!" Hale said.

"Hale? Well, fancy meeting you here." Aloysius Bone, former reporter for the Central Press Syndicate, brushed himself off. He stood about five-five, with dark curly hair and a dark complexion. His light gray suit was not as expensive as Hale's, but the lapels were this year's style. "Thank you for breaking my fall," he said in the soft, ingratiating voice that Hale had always detested. "That gentleman was most ungentlemanly."

"If I'd known it was you, I would have gotten out of the way. What are you doing here? No, let me guess. You want to take over Pike's seat in the bow window. Well, it's not that easy, chump."

After Bone had left the CPS, he had attempted to muscle in on Pike's territory in the gossip line. His reputation as a serious journalist in tatters at the age of just twenty-eight, he was unable to find work with any of the serious papers. But apparently there was plenty of gossip to go around—Baron Kinross's son, Patrick Balfour, was pedaling the same line of garbage under the rather banal pseudonym of "Mr. Gossip." Although Bone had started without the social contacts of a Langdale Pike or Balfour, Hale had heard that he'd done rather well for himself. That didn't elevate the man much in Hale's eyes.

"I just thought I could pick up a tip or two here now that Pike's out of the picture," Bone said. "Management was not sympathetic to that suggestion, however. I don't understand your attitude, old chap. You've got no call to look down on me. I have to make a living, too."

Hale, just under six feet tall, actually couldn't help looking down on the shorter man, literally as well as figuratively. "You're beneath contempt, Aloysius. Everybody in the business knows that Rathbone fired you for making up quotes from the Duke of Glenway."

"Well, he *could* have said it. How was I supposed to know that Rathbone was married to his sister?"

Hale shook his head. "You didn't learn a thing from being fired."

"Climb down a little from your high horse, Hale. Your fine ethics and your Yale degree didn't stop you from getting knocked out the other night, did they?"

Hale grabbed Bone by his appropriately wide lapels. "Where did you hear that?"

"I protect my sources," Bone sniffed.

"Oh, yeah? And who's going to protect you?" Hale did his best to sound like Bulldog Drummond. He judged that his Boston accent rather spoiled the effect, but the implied threat worked well enough on Bone.

"All right, all right. No need to get physical. It's no big secret. I just happened to run into old Harker on the Strand. He told me all about it."

Harker!

"What else did he tell you?"

Bone shrugged. "Just that you're covering Pike's murder, and with your usual tenacity. I already knew that from reading the papers. I saw your story in *The Morning Telegraph*."

Some of the other London papers had slightly rewritten Hale's story and run it without his byline. His archrival Artemis Howell at *The Times* had written his own story with some new but meaningless quotes from Wiggins (". . . several possible lines of inquiry"). But *The Morning Telegraph* had run his story in full without alteration.

Hale let go of Bone's lapels and smoothed them down. "Sorry, Aloysius, I got carried away."

"Nice to see you again, Hale." He skittered away like the White Rabbit.

Bone's unceremonious exit from Arthur's gave Hale pause. He wasn't above using a stratagem to get into a place where a journalist would be unwelcome. Fortunately, he had only recently been the guest of a member.

Just inside the door he encountered an elderly gentleman with hair like cotton and a face wrinkled like a walnut.

"I'd like to speak with Mr. Blanton, please. I'm a friend of a member."

"I shall see if he's available, sir."

Henry Blanton was the manager of Arthur's, the fellow paid to do the bidding of the management committee on a daily basis. Hale had met him once or twice while calling on Pike. After a few minutes of looking at the paintings and statues gracing the foyer, Hale turned to see Blanton striding toward him. The manager was about fifty-five years old, with a large belly and a fringe of gray hair.

"Mr. Hale, isn't it?" He peered out of large glasses.

"That's right, Mr. Blanton. I suppose you recall that I've been here as a guest of Langdale Pike."

"Several times, in fact. Yes, I remember." He shook his head mournfully, like a mortician. "Tragic, his death. Nothing like that has ever happened at Arthur's, never in the more than a hundred years of our existence."

He seemed to take the murder as a personal affront.

"I was wondering if you could answer a few questions," Hale said.

"No, absolutely not," Blanton snapped. "In fact, I'm afraid I'm going to have to ask you to leave."

"Leave? You didn't ask me to leave the last time I was here."

"Two days ago you were a guest. Today you are a reporter."

So Blanton remembered that.

"I'm not a reporter," Hale said. "I'm a journalist."

Blanton's forehead wrinkled. "What's the difference?"

"Reporters don't wear Brooks Brothers suits. Also, the managing director of my news syndicate is the Duke of Glenway's brother-in-law." Hale could see that Blanton was impressed by the name dropping. "And what do you have against reporters, anyway? Pike was a kind of reporter—the worst kind."

"Mr. Pike was a member, as was his father before him. I am sure he would be quite distressed at the commotion his death has caused. The police have been here twice. They've questioned the staff, most particularly Timothy Flood, and they've questioned members. It's a nightmare!"

"That must have been Chief Inspector Wiggins."

"I believe that was the name, yes."

"He's a friend of mine. Wiggins is a fine fellow, but doesn't quite know his place. I'm sure I could make him see how upsetting this is for everyone—and how unnecessary, since surely no one associated with Arthur's could have been responsible for this heinous deed."

For a moment, Hale feared that he'd laid it on too thick. He needn't have worried.

Blanton's eyes widened behind the thick lenses of his glasses. "Could you really do that?"

"Without a doubt." Hale frowned. "But I'm afraid I can't stop the rest of the Press from writing their irresponsible stories as long as this murder remains unsolved. The best thing for Arthur's would be if this case gets cleared up quickly. That would get the murder out of the headlines and people would stop talking about the club as the murder site. You see that, don't you?"

"Yes, I suppose so," Blanton said doubtfully.

"Who's this Timothy Flood fellow that you mentioned?"

"One of our waiters. In point of fact, he served Mr. Pike the fatal cup of tea."

"Tall fellow with blond hair?"

"Yes, sir."

"I recall seeing him on Tuesday. Bad luck for him, getting mixed up in this. But he might know something important without knowing that he knows it. Let's talk to him, shall we?"

Hale thought that a rather smooth way to get an interview with a major witness, but Blanton wasn't fooled.

"Perhaps I have not made myself clear," he said clearly. "Arthur's Club is not seeking any further publicity in this dreadful matter. I'm afraid that I cannot let you speak with members of our staff."

Hale nodded. "Of course. I understand completely. And in honor of my good friend Pike, I want to help you get this unfortunate attention behind you. I've been of assistance to Chief Inspector Wiggins in the past. You remember the Hangman Murders? Well, we worked very closely on that." That was even true, although Hale worked more closely with Sherlock Holmes at the end of the business. "If you let me ask a few questions, perhaps I can help him solve this business and the glaring light of public attention will be removed from Arthur's forever." *Gad, where did that purple prose come from?*

"But you're a re— . . . a journalist."

"True enough, but I promise that nothing your staff tells me will be directly quoted in my story." *Indirectly is another story.* Despite his promise, whatever Hale learned would find its way into print in some form. What was the use of knowing something and not writing it? But the story might wait until he had enough pieces to put together.

After a lingering look at Hale's finely tailored suit, Blanton sighed. "Very well, then. But whatever you do, don't disturb the members. Come with me."

Blanton led Hale through a maze of high-ceilinged rooms. "Timothy should be reporting for work just about now. The waiters have to get here before lunch to learn the specials. He has been quite shaken by this experience. I daresay he feels a certain irrational guilt."

They found the young man in the kitchen. He stood almost as tall as Hale, perhaps five-foot-ten, with strikingly handsome features accented by a dimpled chin. His suit hung a bit loose on his lanky frame. Hale could imagine that he left a trail of broken female hearts all over the Irish neighborhoods of London.

"Timothy, this is Mr. Hale. He'd like to ask you a few questions."

The lad's blue eyes opened wide. "Are you another policeman?" he asked in a thick Irish accent.

"Far from it," Hale assured him. "Don't you remember me? I was sitting with Mr. Pike when he collapsed."

For a moment, Hale thought Timothy Flood was going to do likewise. His jaw dropped and he swayed. "I'm sorry, sir. You could have—"

"No, I don't think so," Hale said with a smile. "I doubt that my Earl Grey was also poisoned." He couldn't be sure, though; his tea had been abandoned in the uproar that followed Pike's demise. "As I remember, you delivered Mr. Pike a special pot—Caribbean Black Sage Tea."

"Yes, sir."

"We procured that variety of tea for Mr. Pike some months ago at his special request," Blanton put it. "Someone told him it was good for what ailed him."

What ailed him was gout, Hale recalled.

"Okay. So when he called for tea you came back here and got the pot. Where was it?"

"Where it always is"—he pointed to the service station—"with all the rest of the pots."

Hale looked around the kitchen. There were a couple of waiters, a scullery-man, a prep-man, and a cook. "Was it any more crowded than this that afternoon?"

"No, sir. About the same."

"So you probably would have noticed if there had been a stranger, somebody you didn't know?"

Was it hope that Hale saw on the young man's chiseled features? "I'm not sure that I would have. I mean, I mind my own business. And I was concentrating on not dropping the pot. So, I wasn't looking around or anything. Maybe there was somebody back here who didn't belong."

Hale nodded. "Right, then. Too bad you didn't notice anyone, but that's still one possibility—an intruder dressed to look like a new cook or waiter. Now, Pike already had the pot of tea sitting in front of him when I arrived. Did anybody else sit down with him before I got there?"

"No, sir."

"Did anybody stand at his table talking to him?"

Blanton blanched. "Surely you don't think that one of our members—" He couldn't even bring himself to finish the horrifying sentence.

"I'm sure other people walk through the doors here—guests, service people, mailmen, and so on," Hale said soothingly.

"Maybe," Timothy said. "Yes, I think I do remember somebody standing there."

"What did he look like?"

"I barely noticed." He paused. "He was shorter than me, I think, with red hair. And dressed in a suit, like everybody else."

"Did you tell Chief Inspector Wiggins this?"

"The copper? No. I never thought of it till just now."

So, Hale thought, I'm a step ahead of Wiggins. *Or maybe not. Maybe I just planted the notion of a man standing next to the teapot in young Timothy Flood's head.* Hale strongly suspected there was plenty of room up there.

"Well, then, that's very clear," Blanton said, facing Hale with a look of triumph on his round face. "This tragedy really had nothing to do with Arthur's. Tell Chief Inspector Wiggins that!"

"You can be sure that I'll be speaking to him."

"Thank you, Timothy. Well done, lad!"

"Me pleasure, Mr. Blanton," said the young Irishman.

Without further commentary, Blanton led the way out of the kitchen. "I hope you're satisfied," he said to Hale.

"Certainly. Well, I do have one more question. What can you tell me about Harrison Scott."

"Nothing." Blanton's voice was flat.

"But he's a member of Arthur's."

"That's why I can tell you nothing. It would be highly inappropriate for me to speak about a member."

"I see. Well, I'll have to ask Mr. Standish then. He's the chairman of the management committee, as I understand."

"You understand correctly. But I sincerely doubt that Mr. Standish will grant you an interview."

"Of course he will, Blanton. Mr. Standish is a politician and I am a journalist. That makes us a natural pair, rather like a dog and a tick."

SEVEN
It Pays to Advertise

"Of course there is *some* truth in advertising. There's yeast
in bread, but you can't make bread with yeast alone."
– Lord Peter Wimsey, *Murder Must Advertise*

Hale spent the rest of the morning and the early
afternoon running into brick walls.

The secretary at G. Standish Shipping Ltd., a steely-
eyed man appropriately named Mr. Frost, informed Hale
that Mr. Standish was at Parliament today seeing to
important affairs of state. And in any case, he added, the
gentleman would have to write in advance if he wished an
appointment.

The important affairs of state must have involved
lunch. At Parliament, where he was not unknown, Hale
learned from a chatty aid that Standish was settled in at one
of the more posh eating establishments nearby and could be
expected to remain there for some time. "You might look
for him at his club this evening," the earnest young man
said. "He usually pops in there around eight-ish. It's
called—"

"Arthur's," Hale said. "I think I can find it. Thank you for the suggestion. You've been most kind."

As he was leaving the hallowed halls of the Mother of Parliaments, he heard a familiar voice rumble, "I say, Hale!" The journalist turned and greeted the rather squat figure of Winston Churchill, Minister for the Colonies. The two were standing in the octagonal Central Hall of Westminster. From here one gained entrance to both houses of Parliament and many halls. Curious, Hale thought, how Churchill's stance fit so well with the statues of past sovereigns and men like Gladstone. But then, he had probably planned it that way.

"I thought you were spending all your time these days writing about criminals," the politician said without bothering to take the cigar out of his mouth. "What are you doing in Parliament?"

"Writing about criminals," Hale quipped.

"Touché!" Churchill laughed heartily. Himself a former journalist, he socialized comfortably with the Press. He particularly seemed to enjoy the company of Hale, who shared his interest in literature and cigars. Their paths had not crossed often since their first meeting two years ago, when Churchill had been Minister for Air and War. But when they did it was always a pleasant happenstance for both. Without asking, Churchill passed Hale a Romeo y Juliet cigar, a brand which he had been smoking ever since he covered the guerilla war in Cuba in 1895.

"I was actually looking for George Standish," Hale said, lighting the cigar.

"Ah, Standish! Good fellow, for a Tory. He shares my taste in Cuban smokes. Standish keeps trying to drag me back to the dark side. We used to belong to the Carlton Club together about twenty years ago."

Churchill had begun his political career as a Tory, but switched to the Liberal Party in 1904. That happened to be at a time when the Liberals were winning elections, cynics observed. But his current party had hit a tough patch just now, and there was speculation that the Conservatives were trying to woo Churchill back with the promise of a brighter future. Churchill was nothing if not ambitious— and opportunistic to boot.

"We have some business dealings, too," Churchill added, "but I won't bore you with that. What brings you into Standish's orbit?"

"A story, of course." Hale explained about Pike's demise, which was no news to Churchill, and his desire to speak with Standish because of his position as chairman of the management committee at Arthur's.

"Alas, poor Pike. I knew him, Hale." The glowering expression on the politician's bulldog face made it clear that to know Pike was not necessarily to love him. "Well, good luck with your story. If I can help, let me know."

"I'll be sure to do that."

After a few more minutes of Hale-fellow-well-met chat, Churchill sent his American friend off with hearty good wishes.

Hale wished that he had gone directly from Arthur's to Benson's. The advertising agency's location in the Kingsway Hall office building at the southwest corner of Kingsway and New Oxford Street was only a little over a mile from St. James's Street. Kingsway was the center of the advertising trade in London because of its nearness to all the newspaper offices on Fleet Street.

On his way there, Hale stopped to see Tom Eliot at Lloyds Bank over on King William Street. The banker dabbled in poetry, very strange poetry, and was up on all things literary. He looked more like a Harvard instructor, which he had once been, than a functionary in the Colonial and Foreign Department at Lloyds. But Hale's hunch that Tom might know something about Benson's proved on the mark.

"Great Britain's largest advertising agency," Eliot informed him, lighting another of his endless French gaspers. Hale considered his affinity for Gauloises among the least of his eccentricities. "They do everything, from small adverts in magazines to large outdoor posters, and they do it quite well. The copy is clever, humorous, and elegant. And their client roster is a like a *Who's Who* of household names—Andrew's Liver Salts, Rowntrees chocolate, Lipton's tea, and the like."

"So what was Benson's name doing in Pike's notebook?"

Eliot smiled behind the thick cigarette smoke. "Perhaps Benson's is at the center of some vast criminal enterprise, like a dope ring."

"You read too many mystery novels." Hale knew that Eliot took a childish delight in them.

"Well, don't say I didn't tell you."

Figuring that an advertising agency wouldn't be adverse to publicity about itself, he presented himself at S.H. Benson Ltd. under his true colors as a reporter for the Central Press Syndicate. His line that he was interested in writing a story about Benson's was only a slight shading of the truth.

"I'm sure that Mr. Benson will be very sorry he missed you," said a female secretary with bleached blond hair, fingering his Central Press Syndicate business card. "I'll ring Mr. Davison, our general manger."

Clive Davison surprised Hale. With a bull neck and regimental mustache, he looked more like a military man than a creative type. But he was chatty enough.

"Actually, we don't especially seek attention for ourselves." He spoke in clipped tones. "The product's the thing, d'you see?"

"I understand perfectly, Mr. Davison. I'm sorry that Benson's won't be included with the other advertising agencies we profile, but if you aren't interested . . ."

Davison interrupted. "I didn't say that. You can't leave us out of a story about the advertising business. We're the biggest fish in the pond. Let's talk in my office. I'm only sorry that Mr. Benson isn't here to speak with you."

"Perhaps I can ask him some follow-up questions later," Hale said helpfully.

Davison's office, sizeable but uncluttered, gave Hale the impression that the money at Benson's wasn't being spent on such frills as decorating. The room held a large desk, a couple of leather chairs in front of it, and, at the opposite end of the room, a round conference table with four smaller chairs. Davison invited Hale to take a seat at the table. Davison sat across from him.

"Can I assume that you know very little about S.H. Benson Ltd.?"

Hale saw an opening. "I just know the name. I think my late friend Mr. Langdale Pike mentioned it once. Did you know him?"

Davison paused, as if thinking, then shook his head. "I don't believe so. Should I have done?"

"Not necessarily, but you could have. He was a journalist of sorts."

"I see. Well, then. Let me start with a little history lesson. Mr. Samuel Herbert Benson founded our firm at 100 Fleet Street in 1893, with Bovril meat extract as his first client. S.H. had formerly managed the Bovril factory for three years. His son Philip, the current Mr. Benson, took over the firm eight years ago. Philip spent some time in America studying new methods of psychological marketing and scientific advertising, which we have now largely adopted."

Davison talked for another twenty-two minutes with all the earnestness of an Oxford don, giving Hale a detailed history of the company up to the present, including its major clients. Hale wrote it all down, and not just for effect. He had no idea what information about Benson's might prove telling.

"Do you have any questions?" Davison asked when he'd finished.

Hale took a shot in the dark. "You must work very closely with your clients."

"Indeed we do! That's one of the secrets of our success. We know them better than they know themselves, and we know their potential customers equally well."

"You must know a lot of their secrets, then."

"What do you mean?"

"I'm not sure, exactly. It's just that, well, if one of the companies you work with, or one of its top people, was doing something a little shady, you'd know it."

Davison frowned. "I don't know what you're driving at, but I can assure you that Benson's adheres to the highest ethical standards, and so do our clients." He stood up. "I think you're finished now."

"Yes, I am," Hale agreed, "but could I get a brief tour of your offices? That would be good for color." And he would be keeping his eyes wide open for anything suspect.

Davison considered that. "I suppose that would be permissible, but you mustn't describe any campaign that's in the works. That's all very confidential, you know."

"Your secrets are safe with me. You have my word."

"All right, then. I'll have one of our new copywriters show you around. She's a woman. We're very progressive here, you see. There were no women in advertising offices before the War, but it's all different now." Hale had the impression that Davison was trying to sound as though he approved of this modern nonsense.

Davison led Hale down a hallway to a small office. Inside sat a woman smoking a cigarette and studying a page proof for an advert, holding it close to her bright blue eyes. She was a plain-looking woman with sparse hair and a long neck. Her red and yellow dress was the brightest thing in the room, but the gold and silver earrings dangling down about three inches from her lobes came in second.

"Miss Sayers?" Davison said. He pronounced the name with two syllables. "I have someone I'd like you to meet."

She stood up quickly, setting down her cigarette in an ashtray and blowing smoke out one side of her mouth. She was tall for a woman, perhaps five-seven, and lanky. Davison quickly introduced Hale to her with a ten-second summary of his mission.

She pumped Hale's hand. "Dorothy L. Sayers," she said briskly in a loud voice, slightly emphasizing the middle initial and giving the last name one syllable.

"I'd like you to give Mr. Hale a look around our offices, give him a feel for what we do here," Davison said. He added, to Hale, "Miss Sayers has only been here a few weeks, but she already has a reputation as one of our bright young girls. She took a first in modern languages from Oxford."

She wasn't *that* young—close to thirty, Hale figured, just a little younger than his thirty-two. And she didn't seem especially pleased at her assignment of playing tour guide to a reporter. But she didn't say so, and Davison quickly disappeared.

"Let's get on with it, then," she said. "Hope you're not bored." She picked the burning cigarette out of the ashtray, sucked hard, and stubbed it while blowing out the smoke.

"Most of the offices on this floor are part of the Literary Department," she said as they walked through. "That's what we call copywriting around here."

Hale chuckled, earning a strong look from Miss Sayers. "Well, it's not as though you're poets, are you?" he said defensively.

"Actually, I am a poet," she said. "My second book of poems was published a few weeks ago."

This isn't going so well, Hale thought. What had happened to his usual success in dealing with women? *It's on a boat to Egypt, Enoch, old man.*

"Most of these offices are empty," Hale said, just to change the subject. "But the tobacco smoke lingers."

"Oh, my ears and whiskers, we're always running around doing things. Lucky you caught me in. Ah, but here's Smythe-Dickey. He's new, too. A gentleman of the Press is visiting us today, Reggie."

They had stopped just outside an office much like Miss Sayers's. A man about Hale's age, dressed in tweeds, looked up from his desk, startled. He had a high forehead and a thin, aristocratic nose. World-weary green eyes, the eyes of a much older man, peered up at Hale through a pair of pince-nez. Somehow he seemed familiar, but if Hale had ever seen him before he couldn't recall when or where.

"Oh, hello." He stood, bringing himself almost on eye-level with Hale. "Reginald Smythe-Dickey."

"Enoch Hale, Central Press Syndicate."

His handshake was not as firm as Dorothy L. Sayers's had been.

"What are you up to, Reggie?" she asked.

"That blasted tooth powder account. I'm working on a poster. What do you think of this: 'Go the extra mile. Brush your teeth with *Smile!*' The second sentence would be a new line, like in a poem."

Miss Sayers frowned. "Not quite there yet."

"Would it be better if I made it a question—you know, 'Why not go the extra mile? Brush your teeth with *Smile!*'"

"I'm sure you'll get it eventually," Miss Sayers said dubiously. "I can never think of tooth powder without remembering that detective story, 'The Problem of Cell 13,' where The Thinking Machine uses tooth powder as part of his escape from prison."

Hale and Smythe-Dickey looked at each other blankly, both unfamiliar with the story.

"I have an idea," Hale said. "How about the name '*Smile*' rather large at the top of the poster, in the same typeface that appears on the product, and then below that a close-up photo of a woman's smile." An unexpected pang hit Hale as he thought of Sadie's mouth, which he had often surveyed in detail. He moved quickly on. "Then below the photo, in parenthesis, 'The name says it all.'"

"Bung-ho, that's actually rather good!" Smythe-Dickey said. He frowned. "But if you have to say, 'the name says it all,' then the name didn't really say it all, did it? I mean, if the name said it all, the only thing on the poster would be the name, wouldn't it?"

"Yes, I see what you mean," said Hale, thoroughly confused. "I suppose I'd better stick to journalism."

He and his tour guide soon moved on to Benson's other departments.

"Your idea really wasn't bad," Dorothy said at one point, lighting another cigarette. By now they had become "Dorothy" and "Enoch" to each other. "I should say you have more of a future in advertising than Smythe-Dickey."

"What's wrong with him?"

"Other than lack of talent? His nerves seem rather shot, for one thing. I think he was ruined by the World War; so many men were. But there's something else strange about him, something deceptive. He's not what he seems. I think he bears watching."

"You read a lot of detective stories, don't you? Sexton Blake and all that."

"Doesn't everybody with a brain?"

"I had a friend who was rather closely associated years ago with a real-life detective—Sherlock Holmes."

Dorothy's eyes sparkled with interest. "How delicious!"

"Yes. My friend's name was Langdale Pike." He had planned to look closely for a reaction, but he didn't have to. Dorothy's response wasn't subtle.

She chuckled. "You mean like the peaks in the Lake District? What an odd name."

So neither Clive Davison nor Dorothy L. Sayers had ever heard of Pike. At least, that's what he was supposed to believe.

EIGHT
Suspicions

"Why, sometimes I've believed as many as six impossible
things before breakfast."
> – The White Queen, *Through the Looking-Glass*

Dorothy Leigh Sayers—she was always proud of the
Leigh family—in truth had remembered seeing the name of
Langdale Pike in two newspaper stories, the latest just that
morning. And both had carried the byline of Enoch Hale.
This, too, she recalled immediately upon being introduced
to the tall American.

Why she hadn't said so she could not have
explained even to herself, then or later. But a turn of mind
shaped by her preference for detective fiction may have had
something to do with it.

At lunchtime, having a bit to eat and a pint at the
Museum Tavern across from the British Museum, she lit a
cigarette and reread the story in *The Morning Telegraph* under
the blaring headline:

JOURNALIST'S DEATH CALLED MURDER

By Enoch Hale
Central Press Syndicate

The unexpected death earlier this week of a well-known London journalist was due to homicide rather than a heart attack, according to Scotland Yard.

"It has been established that Mr. Langdale Pike died of poisoning by prussic acid," said Chief Inspector Henry Wiggins of the Metropolitan Police. "It was probably administered in his tea."

There are no suspects at this time, according to Wiggins, but he said the investigation has just begun.

Pike, a purveyor of stories to the sensational press and a habitué of Arthur's Club for more than 20 years, died Tuesday while drinking tea at the club with this writer.

Dorothy was quite capable of believing up to six impossible things before breakfast—she was rather fond of the White Queen—but Enoch Hale's appearance at Benson's being a coincidence wasn't one of them. It had something to do with Pike's death, Dorothy was sure. The man wasn't sent out by his editors to write a feature story on advertising agencies two days after seeing a murder carried out literally right under his nose.

Was Enoch investigating Smythe-Dickey? Someone ought to! There was definitely something fishy about that man. She couldn't say so to that Wiggins person, of course. She'd get the same treatment she had got from Enoch: "You read a lot of detective stories, don't you?" *Men!* They never really thought that women were quite human, not even those men who considered themselves very modern. She exhaled cigarette smoke vigorously.

Still . . . she lingered over pleasant thoughts of Enoch Hale. He was so *American*. Dorothy considered love a game, and it was a game in which Hale would be quite a worthy opponent. He might at last be the man to her measure. It didn't hurt a bit that he was handsome as the devil and just as charming. She'd have to find out more about him—whether he was married, for instance. And she knew just the person to ask . . .

To be quite fair, Enoch had been right: she *did* read a lot of detective stories. She loved Philips Oppenheim, Edgar Wallace, G.K. Chesterton, E.C. Bentley, Sexton Blake, Wilkie Collins . . .

She'd even written her own mystery novel, for which she had great hopes. *The Singular Adventure of the Man with the Golden Pince-Nez* was about an unknown body found in someone's bathtub. She'd gotten the idea from a game of "Murder" back when she was a student at Somerville College in Oxford. As Dorothy earned four pounds a week at Benson's, it pleased her to make her amateur sleuth, Lord Peter Wimsey, quite wealthy indeed. But he was no superman. He was rather short, several inches shorter than Enoch. And he suffered from bad nerves as a result of his service in the Great War, like her friend Eric Whelpton . . . and perhaps Reginald Smythe-Dickey.

Dorothy stubbed her cigarette with a sigh. Unfortunately, Lord Peter wasn't here to deal with this Smythe-Dickey business. What was the man up to? Perhaps he was part of a white slave ring based out of Benson's! As much as Dorothy loved the idea, it seemed unlikely. Smythe-Dickey had only arrived at Benson's a little before her, and he seemed too much of a loner to be part of a conspiracy.

Hale was investigating, that couldn't be plainer. Maybe he would come up with something. But she couldn't just sit back and see what he came up with.

What would Sexton Blake do? More to the point, what would Lord Peter Wimsey do?

NINE
A Hint of Scandal

At every word a reputation dies.
    – Alexander Pope, *The Rape of the Lock*

Inconclusive, Hale decided on his way to his office. That was the best way so sum up his visit to S.H. Benson Ltd. There were so many ways to account for the fact that Pike had written "S.H. Benson's" in his notebook, and yet no one there had reacted to Pike's name. Did that mean he was unknown there—or known so well that the connection had to be denied?

Maybe Pike had actually meant S.H. Benson, the person. Was he still alive, though no longer running the business? Hale didn't know. Neither Eliot nor Davison had mentioned that. Or maybe Pike had jotted down the name as something to check out, but never gotten around to it. Or maybe whoever he was interested in at Benson's—if it was a person—wasn't someone that Hale had met. Or maybe Clive Davison and Dorothy Sayers did know Pike but lied about it. Maybe the whole firm was crooked.

Maybe, maybe, maybe!

It didn't seem likely that a newcomer, such as Dorothy or Reginald Smythe-Dickey, would have been the focus of Pike's attention. Or did it? Maybe someone new to Benson's—a change in the equation—was exactly why Pike had written down the name of the firm, and what he wanted to talk to Hale about. Dorothy had insisted that there was something suspect about the improbably named Smythe-Dickey. (Who would make up such a moniker?) Perhaps he did warrant a closer look. But Dorothy was a new hire at the advertising agency, too. What if she was up to something and was trying to throw suspicion in another direction?

Hale had found the woman intriguing, he had to confess to himself with a twinge of guilt. With her plain looks, long neck, and gawky manner, she was nowhere near as attractive as his beloved Sadie. And yet her brash exuberance did attract Hale. She was obviously smart, too—an Oxford graduate, Davison had said. Although women had studied at Oxford colleges for a long time, they'd only been granted official degrees for a couple of years.

Such were Hale's musings when he arrived at Fleet Street to find the office in an uproar. The Irish Republican Army had assassinated Field Marshal Sir Henry Wilson on the street in front of his home. This was a major story, coming at a time when the new Irish Free State government was supposed to be getting the IRA under control. Hale felt certain that His Majesty's Secret Service, about which he knew more than he would like, must be very busy looking for conspirators. Ned Malone was assigned to write the main story, but Hale dashed off some of the sidebars.

For some hours, then, Dorothy was not on his mind. Thoughts of her returned to him, however, as he walked down St. James's Street toward Arthur's that evening. Hale suspected that her poetry would be interesting, and undoubtedly more understandable than Eliot's. He resolved to try to find a copy.

The near-darkness of the quiet street reminded him of the attack on him and the theft of Pike's notebook two nights before. Even as that memory entered his head, Hale noticed the sound of footsteps behind him. *Nothing unusual about that.* He turned and saw a loafer in baggy pants and a flat cap looking through a shop window. *Just nerves.* This business was getting to him more than he'd realized. He shook it off and kept walking.

Within a few more minutes he presented himself to the front door attendant at Arthur's. He was a stout fellow with gray hair and a welcoming disposition.

"I have an appointment with Mr. Standish," he lied.

"Your name, sir?"

"Lord—oh, just tell him Enoch Hale."

The functionary returned a few minutes later, smile still firmly in place. "Mr. Standish is in the dining room having his supper, sir. He asks you to join him there. Please follow me."

Standish was already eating at a table beneath a huge painting of a British king. Hale was fairly certain the monarch was George III, the last ruler of the American colonies. By comparison, George Standish, O.B.E., M.P., looked quite ordinary in his double-breasted gray pinstriped suit. He was about forty, maybe a little younger, with black hair parted in the middle and a mustache much thicker than Hale's. He hadn't yet put on the extra pounds, but that would come in a few years.

He looked up at Hale from his rack of lamb. "You've got a nerve, *Lord* Hale, saying you have an appointment with me. Well, don't just stand there. Sit down."

Hale obeyed, saying nothing. He had learned that silence was one of the best tricks of the journalist's trade. People tend to be uncomfortable with silence, so they fill it with their own words. Some of the best quotes in his stories had come in response to silence rather than to questions.

"I'm used to dealing with your kind, the Press," Standish said. "It's an occupational hazard for a public man. Yes, I recognized your name. Central Press Syndicate, isn't it? Pike seemed to think you were a fine fellow. But you haven't got yourself off on a very good footing with me. What do you have to say for yourself?"

Hale opted for the bold approach, hoping to win Standish's respect if not his affection. "I guess I should start by saying I'm sorry, but I won't do that because I'm not."

"Is the gentleman ready to order?"

Hale looked up to see an elderly waiter, rather bent, with a white goatee.

"I don't—" Hale began.

"We'll both have the nutmeg custard tart," Standish said. "And coffee."

The waiter smiled. "A fine choice, gentlemen."

When he'd left, Standish said, "You may now continue hanging yourself."

"I was about to say that I'm not sorry for doing the only thing I could think of to get to see you, Mr. Standish. I tried your office and I tried Parliament. Your club was the only option left."

Standish sighed, pushing away his empty plate. "Time was when a man's club was sacrosanct. Nobody would bother him there. I wish I'd been born a hundred years earlier. Well, you certainly have been persistent, Hale; I must admit that. I suppose you want to talk to me about poor Pike, but I don't know any more about his demise than you do—probably much less."

"You met with him shortly before he died, didn't you?"

"How the devil did you know that?"

"Come now, Mr. Standish, you know we reporters don't reveal our sources." With an inward cringe, Hale realized that he sounded all too much like Aloysius Bone. "What did you two talk about?"

"That's none of your business. I can assure you that it had nothing to do with Pike's murder."

"You can't know that."

Hale let that sink in while the waiter came over and poured coffee.

"You don't know why he was killed, do you?" he said after the waiter had gone.

"No, of course not."

"Then you can't know that your conversation had nothing to do with it."

After a pause, Standish said, "Very well, then. Pike rang me up and asked to meet with me in my capacity as chairman of the management committee of Arthur's. He said he had to talk about a very sensitive matter."

"When was that? I mean, when did you meet?"

"The day he died, about ten in the morning. We talked for about fifteen or twenty minutes."

Hale wasn't sure exactly what time Pike had summoned him to Arthur's, but it was before eleven o'clock. Was the timing just a coincidence, or was there a connection between Pike's meeting with Standish and the former's desire to speak with Hale?

"What was the sensitive matter?"

Standish looked distinctly uncomfortable. "When I say that it was a sensitive matter, I mean that it was one that it wouldn't be appropriate for me to discuss with anyone else."

He sat back as the waiter set down the tarts. The pause gave Hale a few moments to think about how to approach this.

"I understand that you're worried about the reputation of the club," he said finally. "I assure you that whatever you tell me will be strictly off the record. I won't write about it, but it may help me with my inquiries."

Standish gave a sardonic smile. "It is not my experience that journalists with exclusive information, especially anything containing a hint of scandal, refrain from reporting it."

"I can be trusted. Ask Winston Churchill."

"Churchill!"

"We're in the way of being friends."

"The devil you say! Well, that's a point in your favor. Churchill may be a rank opportunist, but he's no fool. In fact, his judgment is quite sound in most matters. He certainly knew how to deal with the Irish." In December 1919, Hale remembered, Churchill had been one of the driving forces recruiting demobilized soldiers to augment the Royal Irish Constabulary. They became known, and dreaded in Ireland, as the Black and Tans because of their uniform. Churchill had also joined his friend Lord Arthur Balfour—known as "Bloody Balfour" for his service as Chief Secretary of Ireland late in the last century—in pushing hard for the execution of Sir Roger Casement for treason after the Easter Rising of 1916.

Hale ate his tart, which was very good, saying nothing. Standish leaned forward and spoke in a lower voice. "All right, I'll take the risk and tell you. Pike had become aware of a sodomite relationship involving a member. I won't tell you his name. That kind of thing could ruin a man and do the club no good."

That was certainly true. "The love that dare not speak its name," as Lord Alfred Douglas had called it a generation ago, was no more acceptable now than it had been in the days of Oscar Wilde's imprisonment and subsequent early death. Casement's lurid "Black Diaries," detailing his homosexual promiscuity, had completely undermined attempts to save him from the hangman's rope. "What did you do with this information?" Hale asked.

"I spoke to the member and suggested a quiet resignation. I am given to understand that will happen within the month."

"I guess Pike's report about the man was true, then."

The story of Pike going to Standish with the tale sounded plausible, but Hale had been around long enough to realize that the opposite was equally likely: The esteemed Member of Parliament sitting in front of him may well have actually *given* this information to Pike in order to destroy the club member involved, who was probably a political enemy. That kind of gossip was Pike's stock in trade. He was at least as likely to be receiving such news as giving it out. And when he gave it out, it was more likely to be in print than in a discreet meeting with the chairman of the management committee.

"What can you tell me about a member of Arthur's named Harrison Scott?" Hale asked.

Standish raised his eyebrows almost comically. "Scott? Good Lord, what could he have to do with this mess?"

"I have no idea. I just heard his name in a context that made me wonder who he is."

"What context?" Standish pressed.

"I'd rather not say."

Standish regarded the American coldly as he drank from his cup. "Trust is a two-way street, Hale. I told you more than I should have. I think you owe me."

Only later did Hale realize how strange it was that an O.B.E. and Member of Parliament should be calling in chits from an ex-pat American reporter—make that "journalist"—working for the world's fourth-ranked news service.

"All right, then," he said. "It's just that I heard—never mind where; it doesn't matter—that Pike talked with Harrison Scott in the days before he died."

Standish chuckled. "Is that all?" He poured himself another cup of coffee from a silver pot. "Members talk to each other all the time. This is a social club, not the Diogenes, for heaven's sake!"

"Point taken." Hale had once been transported by force to the Diogenes Club, whose members were forbidden to speak to each other except in the Strangers Room. The experience was not among his fondest memories. "Still, what can you tell me about Scott?"

"Not a lot." Standish and Hale both sipped their coffee for a few moments as Standish thought about it. "He's the sort of person who disappears in a crowd. If you saw him on the train or on the street, you'd never notice him. I couldn't even give you a good description. As I recall, he has some position in Whitehall that has a long name and a small office. I suspect he does important but boring work. He's a rather boring individual. We are off the record aren't we?"

Hale left Arthur's soon after, thanking Standish for the information and the tart.

Shortly after he turned right at the bottom of the marble steps, he once again had the feeling that he was being followed. He stopped. Footsteps behind him stopped when he did. He judged the sound to be about half a block behind him. He walked on until he was half a block beyond the street lamp, so that his pursuer would be in the light. Slowing down but not stopping again, he pulled out a pocket watch that he had won from his friend Hemingway in a wartime poker game in Italy. Holding the relatively large watch in his palm without opening it, he used the silver cover like a mirror to look behind him. He wasn't one hundred percent sure that the vague figure he saw reflected there was the idler in the flat cap from earlier in the evening, but close enough.

He walked on for another block, then turned right onto Little St. James's Street. He ducked into the first doorway he saw and waited for his shadow. Sure enough, the figure in the cap walked past him. He was a slight fellow. Without a cosh in his hand and the element of surprise, he would be no match for Hale.

Hale came up behind the stranger, his fists clenched and ready for action. "Looking for me?"

The figure whirled around. "No, I'm following you," came the cheerful reply. "I just don't seem to be doing a very good job of it, do I? I hope you haven't forgotten me already, Mr. Hale?"

Hale released the tensions in his fists. "Oh, I very much doubt that I could ever forget you, Miss Sayers."

TEN
Playing Sleuth

Man is an imitative creature.
      – J.C.F. Schiller, *Wallenstein's Death*

In bizarre circumstances, one is susceptible to bizarre thoughts. So it was that Enoch Hale, face to face with Dorothy L. Sayers dressed as a man, found himself thinking of a woman he'd never met. At the time of the Hangman Murders, he had given himself a crash course in Dr. Watson's accounts of Sherlock Holmes's adventures. The first of the shorter reports, titled "A Scandal in Bohemia," had told how the notorious adventuress and sometime opera singer Irene Adler had bested Holmes in a battle of wits. In one scene of that little drama, she had followed Holmes while dressed in male garb. So Hale couldn't give Dorothy's disguise any points for originality, especially since he wasn't in a generous mood.

"Just what the hell are you up to?" he demanded.

She lit a cigarette. "That's just what I wanted to ask you, but I was quite certain you wouldn't tell me. Ergo, I followed you. I'm devastated that I made such a hash of it."

"Why do you care what I'm up to?"

"I know who you are and I know that you're covering Langdale Pike's murder for your syndicate. I'm sure that's why you were at Benson's. I was hoping to find that you took me seriously when I said there's something not quite right about Smythe-Dickey. Instead you returned to the scene of the crime. Isn't that what murderers are supposed to do?"

Hale ignored the question. He shook his head, still stuck on the fact that she put on male clothing and followed him. "Of all the melodramatic stunts . . ."

"It's what Lord Peter would have done."

As an American, Hale found noble titles more off-putting than impressive. "Who's that—some friend of yours with more money than sense?"

Dorothy assumed a haughty air as she blew smoke. "He has plenty of sense. And he's more than a friend. I rather think I'm going to fall in love with the man."

"Oh. I see." The declaration hit Hale with a pang that he desperately wanted to avoid examining too closely. Who was she to him, anyway? He barely knew her.

"Actually, you don't see. Peter Wimsey is an amateur sleuth of my own invention. I've written a mystery novel about him which I hope to get published."

Hale surprised himself by saying, "I think you should come with me."

"Come where?" she asked warily. "I warn you—"

"Murray's Night Club. It couldn't be more public. Your virtue, if any, will be perfectly safe. I'd like you to meet a friend of mine. More important, I'd like him to meet you. You seem to have a lot in common."

Most London nightclubs closed in the summer heat, but Murray's had an OZONAIR cooling system that enabled it to stay open year-round. Started by American Jack Mays and Englishman Ernest Cordell in 1911 to capitalize on the tango craze, Murray's was regarded as the hub of the English dancing world. From the outside front it looked like a bank, but the ballroom held four hundred guests. The food, drinks, music, and cabaret shows were of the highest caliber.

Hale met Tom Eliot there for drinks once or twice a week, a habit they'd fallen into shortly after Hale arrived in London. Tom had known his cousin, Emily Hale, back at Harvard. Hale was fairly sure he'd "known" her in the biblical sense, but a gentleman never tells—and Tom Eliot was nothing if not a gentleman.

"He's married to an English woman," Hale told Dorothy on the way, "but they don't get along. I think he goes to Murray's to get away from her."

They found Eliot parked behind a martini and a cloud of cigarette smoke from his Gauloises. He lifted his eyebrows when he saw Hale. *Probably wondering what I'm doing with another female just after Sadie left the country*, Hale thought guiltily. Or maybe Eliot was just wondering why this strange woman was wearing a man's shirt, pants, and cap.

"This is my new Bohemian friend Dorothy L. Sayers," Hale said. "She works at Benson's, but she plays at writing poetry and detective stories. I thought you'd like to meet her. Oh, Dorothy, I neglected to mention that Tom writes poetry when he's not doing whatever he does in foreign accounts at Lloyds Bank."

"A banker-poet? How charming!" She spoke in her usual loud voice. Hale thought that she would probably speak in her loud voice at a funeral or in a library. "Did you know that there's another American poet named Eliot?"

"Actually, I don't think there is," Eliot said mildly.

"I'm sure of it." Hale suspected that Dorothy was sure of everything. "He's the author of—Wait a tick. Are you Thomas *Stearns* Eliot?"

"Guilty, my dear."

"Oh, I adore your work! 'Prufrock' was brilliant! I loved the name."

"I wish I could say I made it up, but there was a furniture store called Prufrock's in St. Louis when I was a child."

Hale could make neither heads nor tails out of "The Love Song of J. Alfred Prufrock," which Eliot had written some years before. And that was supposed to be some of his best stuff.

Eliot went on to tell Dorothy that he had just finished a much longer poem called "The Waste Land," which he planned to publish in a few months in a new magazine he was starting. Dorothy seemed enthralled. *Maybe*, Hale thought, *I should have just given her a swat and sent her home instead of bringing her here.* His mind drifted back to the night he'd met Sadie at the scene of the first Hangman Murder. Already smitten, he'd brought her to Murray's after her performance at the Alhambra Music Hall. They'd talked and danced until the early hours of the morning.

"So what did you find out at Benson's?" Eliot asked Hale abruptly, interrupting the reverie.

"I found out that they have a female copywriter who is a buttinski," he said. "Miss Sayers here followed me to Arthur's, where I had an interview with George Standish, the chairman of the management committee."

"He caught me," Dorothy said brightly.

"This sounds like a story worth hearing," Eliot said. "Why don't you tell me everything that's happened since you left my office this morning, Hale?"

Without quite making a conscious decision to trust Dorothy, Hale began his account by filling her in on the stolen notebook and what he remembered of its contents. For her part, to Hale's surprise, Dorothy kept quiet during the entire recital. Their drinks—another martini with Booth's gin for Eliot, a Manhattan for Hale, and a Scotch and soda for Dorothy—were delivered just as Hale finished bringing the other two up to date.

"The killer obviously either knows or suspects that Pike's notebook contains something incriminating to him," Dorothy said.

"Well, Hale has established that some member of Arthur's has a nasty little secret," Eliot said. "That's a juicy motive for murder."

"Don't be silly." Dorothy waved the notion away along with her cigarette smoke. Hale wondered idly how anyone could smoke something called "Whifflets." "That would never pass muster in any of the better detective stories. To kill the man after he's blown the whistle to the chairman of the management committee would be closing the barn door after the cow has run away. There would be no point in it."

"On the contrary," Eliot said, "being dead would keep Pike from writing about it."

"If he were going to write about it, he wouldn't have told Standish first," Dorothy said.

"But maybe the killer didn't know that he told Standish," Hale objected.

Dorothy ignored that. "It does make perfect sense, however, that Pike was killed to keep him from writing something. After all, that's what he did. London society is littered with the walking dead who were subjects of Pike's paragraphs in the trash papers. Maybe Pike saw something happen across the street from his spot in the bow window at Arthur's, something that would be devastating to someone's reputation if he wrote about it. That's what it would be in a Sexton Blake story!"

The idea sounded a bit far-fetched to Hale, rather like—well, like a Sexton Blake story. He'd always regarded Blake, the hawk-nosed British private detective, as a shameless fictionalization of the real-life Sherlock Holmes. Blake even lived on Baker Street.

"Being a woman," Dorothy steamed on, "I've never found occasion to venture into Clubland. What would Pike be able to see from that bow window where you said he always sat?"

"Well, there's a coincidence," Eliot said with a nervous laugh. "We—Lloyds, I mean—have a big granite office building on the northwest corner of St. James's and King Streets. But it's partially demolished for renovation right now."

"Pike had a perfect view of the Motor Union Insurance Company on the southeast corner," Hale offered. "I think the address is 10 King Street."

"That doesn't sound very promising," Dorothy admitted. "Of course, he might have seen anything on the street—the Prince of Wales buying cocaine, for all we know. But there's no way we'll ever find that out. Anyone else who saw the same thing either didn't realize what was going on or has already taken action."

"'We'?" Hale repeated. "You said 'we.' When did we become 'we'?"

"When you insisted that I come here with you. It wasn't my idea." Despite himself, Hale was impressed at the facile way she made it sound as though she'd been dragged kicking and screaming into this business. The man's flat cap she still wore told a different story. "Anyway, forget the bow window. It's a marvelous theory, but as unlikely as it is unprovable. The truth is much simpler. I bet that Pike knew something about Reggie Smythe-Dickey that he couldn't be allowed to report."

Eliot's eyebrows came together in concentration. Although Hale gave no credence to Dorothy's fantasies about the other new copywriter at Benson's, he had mentioned them in his summary of the day's researches.

"The trash papers wouldn't be interested in whatever that man's foibles might be," Hale objected. "He's a nobody."

"We don't know that," Dorothy said. "We don't know who he really is. Perhaps he's a somebody pretending to be a nobody."

"For what purpose?" Eliot said. "And why at Benson's?"

"Aye, there's the rub," Dorothy admitted. "I haven't been there long, but it's hard to see Philip Benson or Clive Davison running a dope ring out of the agency."

"I'm sure you'll keep your eyes open and inform us if you see anything suspicious along that line," Hale said dryly. "Meanwhile, I think I'd best move on to the other names I remember from Pike's notebook—that rather shadowy Harrison Scott fellow and G.K. Chesterton."

"Good old G.K.C.!" Dorothy said. "I fell in love with his writing at college and I never fell out of it. I saw him in person once, when he came to Somerville as a guest lecturer about eight years ago. What could he possibly have to do with a man like Langdale Pike?"

"That's what I intend to ask him," Hale said.

Eliot set down his empty martini glass and cleared his throat theatrically. "This has been very entertaining, in the best tradition of *Trent's Last Case*. But for all our fine speculation, you know full well it's much more likely that Pike was killed for some boring domestic reason that had nothing to do with a deep, dark secret or his notebook. If you're going to stick your nose around, Hale, you ought to stick it into Pike's family."

"He was a bachelor," Hale said. "Apparently his sister ran his household, a woman named Lydia Grayson. I presume she's a widow. I've tried several times to talk to her. I'll keep trying. But tomorrow I plan to visit Chesterton."

ELEVEN
The Paradoxical Mr. Chesterton

The Bible tells us to love our neighbors, and also to love
our enemies; probably because they are generally the
same people.
> – G. K. Chesterton

"Capital!" Rathbone proclaimed in a withering tone.
"You're only missing one thing."

"What's that?" Hale asked.

"A story!"

It was Wednesday morning, three days after the
murder, and Hale had just finished debriefing Rathbone on
his adventures of the day before. They were in the
managing director's office with the door closed, safe from
the prying ears, if not eyes, of Horace Harker.

"I hope you haven't lost sight of the fact that this is
a news service," Rathbone continued. "Our clients expect
us to deliver all day every day, Hale. You very unwisely
boxed yourself in with a promise not to report what
Standish told you about his meeting with Pike. And what
have you got to show for it?"

Hale thought quickly. "I still think that deal will pay off later. Standish may have given us the key to the whole business." *Or maybe not.* "Meanwhile, I could dash off a quick feature on Benson's, the king of the British advertising agencies. I have some good quotes from Clive Davis, the managing director, and a very clever copywriter named Dorothy L. Sayers."

The South African appeared skeptical. "A woman with a middle initial?"

"She insists on it."

Rathbone fiddled with his curved pipe, considering. "No," he said finally, "I told you that you're on the Pike murder and I want you to stay on it."

That was a good thing, because Hale had already made arrangements to visit G.K. Chesterton at his home in Beaconsfield. G.K.C. had removed his famous figure from London more than a decade earlier, choosing to work instead from a home in the country. But Beaconsfield was less than twenty-four miles northwest of Charing Cross.

Among all his other protean efforts, Chesterton had been writing his *Illustrated London News* column every week since 1905. In a brief conversation on the telephone, Hale had appealed to the author's well-known self-identification as a journalist.

"I know this is a bit of a bother," he'd said, surprising himself by how British he had begun to sound, "but we're up against a deadline and my boss insists that I talk to you for this follow-up story about the murder of Langdale Pike. It would really be a big help if you'd see me. Otherwise, I'm going to get in trouble."

"Trouble, eh?" the great man rumbled. "Well, we can't have that. Come ahead, then. I'll see you around lunch time." He gave directions.

Chesterton had expressed no surprise at Pike's name, as he most likely would have if he hadn't known the man. That encouraged Hale.

Whether the interview advanced his story or not, an hour or so with one of Britain's most prominent men of letters and original thinkers promised to be fascinating. Hale whistled a cheerful tune as he left the building an hour later—until the sight of a woman standing on the front walk stopped him in mid-whistle.

"You again!" he exclaimed.

"Oh, there you are. Finally. Ready to go?"

Dorothy L. Sayers, decked out in a bright orange dress, puffed on a cigarette.

"Go? What do you mean?" Hale felt as though he'd entered the second act of a farce without having seen the first act.

"Well, surely you didn't think you'd pay a call on G.K.C. without me, did you? I told you how much I admire him."

After a moment of stunned silence, Hale said, "How did you know he'd agree to see me?"

"I'm sure you can be very persuasive. Besides, he's a soft touch."

Hale began walking briskly. "As it happens, he did agree to see *me*. I didn't tell him I'd be bringing an entourage."

Dorothy stretched her legs to keep up with Hale's pace. "He won't mind."

"Shouldn't you be at your desk at Benson's writing an advert for, I don't know, Guinness or something?"

"I'm on the sick." She coughed dramatically.

"He lives in Beaconsfield, you know. I'm taking the train."

"I can afford the ticket. Let's ride to the station on my motorcycle."

It was hopeless. The woman was like flypaper. At least she wasn't dressed like a man this morning.

"We'll walk," Hale said.

As they headed toward Charing Cross Station, he asked Dorothy to tell him about "this amateur sleuth in your mystery novel."

"Lord Peter? First of all, he's quite wealthy. I think in the next book I shall give him a new sports car. Why not? It costs me nothing."

It turned out that her own finances before taking the job at Benson's were such that her father, a country parson, had paid to have the manuscript of her book typed. Hale hoped that the supremely self-confident Dorothy wouldn't be too crushed when her magnum opus of mystery didn't find a publisher. Half the reporters and editors he knew had at least one unpublished manuscript tucked away in a desk drawer.

The train ride passed pleasantly enough as they chatted along. That was the trouble. Poor Sadie was still steaming toward Egypt, where she would spend months with mummies and the even more desiccated Alfie Barrington. It just wasn't fair for Hale to be enjoying himself. But he was.

From mysteries the conversation moved on to poetry, *Alice in Wonderland*, jazz (Dorothy played the saxophone), photography, crossword puzzles, Christianity, and music halls. Time flew by like the telephone poles glimpsed from the train window. Before Hale knew it they were in Beaconsfield.

The house on Grove Road recently bought by Gilbert and Frances Chesterton was a red brick dwelling with a machine tile roof, just one story plus an attic. A gabled addition was underway.

A woman with plain features and short hair answered the door. And yet her face wasn't so plain at that, Hale realized. While not pretty, it showed determination and character.

"Oh, yes, he told me earlier that you were coming, although he may have forgotten by now," the woman said when Hale had introduced himself. "He's a bit absent-minded about practical matters. I'm Frances, his wife. He's in the library."

Even without his familiar props—the broad-brimmed hat, the swordstick, the cape—a good portion of the British public would have recognized the ample girth, the big mustache, and the mane of hair that was Gilbert Keith Chesterton. Perhaps the same could even be said in the United States, where he had gone on a successful speaking tour in 1920–21.

Chesterton sat at a library desk, writing with a fountain pen. When Hale and Dorothy entered the room, he rose from his chair. Towering a good five inches over Hale's five-foot-eleven and then some, he extended his hand in greeting. "I had a vague notion that we were having a guest today. But I wasn't expecting two of you."

"Neither was I," said Hale dryly. "Thanks again for seeing *us.*"

Dorothy was uncharacteristically quiet. From the look on her face, Hale could tell that she was as much in awe of the legendary G.K.C. as she had been as a Somerville college student all those years ago.

"Well, then, tell me what this is all about and we'll see if we can make your editor happy," Chesterton said, lowering his bulk into a chair. "Afterwards, we'll have a spot of lunch with Frances." He stuck a cigar in his mouth.

"You're very kind," Hale said. "As you know, I was with Pike when he died and I've been reporting on his murder. According to a notebook he kept, he had an appointment with you a few days before his murder."

Chesterton nodded his leonine head. "Yes, it was on Friday, a week ago tomorrow. I'm not always good on such details, but I remember that. I was in London to meet with my book publisher just around the corner from Arthur's, so I called Langdale the day before and told him I'd be stopping by."

"What for?" Dorothy asked, speaking for the first time.

Chesterton regarded her through his pince-nez with a look of puzzlement. "Why, we were friends, of course."

"If I may be so bold," Hale said, "you and Pike wouldn't seem to have had much in common."

"Oh, we had nothing in common except a profound disagreement with each other. We argued about religion— he had none—politics, and economic theory. I shall miss that very much. I've been praying for his soul, which he didn't believe in."

"So this wasn't a meeting with an agenda. Do you remember what you talked about?"

"Certainly. Langdale, not uniquely among my secular friends, expended a great deal of energy taking me to task for my reception into the Catholic Church this past Eastertide. This attitude continues to puzzle me greatly. If a heretic of my acquaintance abandoned one heresy for another, I don't see why I would take sides. One heresy is as good as another. Shouldn't an atheist think that one religion is as good as another?"

"Why did you do it?" Dorothy asked. "Join the Roman Church, I mean."

"I had no choice, my dear. I didn't claim Catholicism; Catholicism claimed me. After I wrote a book called *Orthodoxy* some years ago, what else could I do but eventually become orthodox, small 'o'? I now seem to have offended my friends and foes equally. And whether my fellow communicants are happy to have me worshipping among them I would not hazard a guess. I only know that I have made myself happy and, I hope, God."

"I think the Catholics are right about everything except the primacy of the pope," Dorothy said. "And I much prefer the R.C. clergy, especially Father Brown, to the Anglicans."

Chesterton smiled. "The pope's infallibility on matters of doctrine, I take on faith. My own fallibility, I know from experience. Therefore I should much prefer his judgment to mine, which is not to say that I don't have any."

"I'll say," Hale muttered. Chesterton had judgments on everything, and expressed them forcefully and often epigrammatically in his unending stream of essays and books. They even crept into his mystery novels and Father Brown short stories, although artfully enough that they didn't spoil Hale's enjoyment in reading them.

But this whole conversation was straying far from the purpose of Hale and Dorothy's trip to Beaconsfield. Hale tried to pull it back with a question. "Do you have any idea who would want to kill Pike?"

Chesterton puffed on his cigar for a moment. "That's rather beside the point, isn't it? The bookseller he jostled on the street that morning might have wanted to kill him, but he didn't. So many people hated him that the only sensible suspect is the woman who loved him."

"His sister, you mean?"

"I mean the woman he lived with. In the futile hope of scandalizing me, Langdale made a point of affirming on several occasions that she was not in fact his sister, nor did they live together as brother and sister."

TWELVE
So Many Suspects

There is no cure for slander.
– Danish proverb

Dorothy was far from shocked to learn that Langdale Pike had lived with a woman who was neither his sister nor his wife. The minister's daughter had moved in Bohemian circles during most of her adult life. More than one earnest young man had lectured her hopefully, but not persuasively, about "free love"—as if love could ever come without price. Since the Great War, and the moral chaos that followed, even this philosophical fig leaf had been dropped by many in the mad rush to experience.

Perhaps the biggest surprise was that Pike bothered to conceal the nature of his relationship with Lydia Grayson from the world at large. But he was of an older generation and moved among the sort of men who belonged to Arthur's. Many of them had mistresses, she was sure, but discreetly; they didn't exactly hire Benson's to advertise it.

"I realize that you've already tried without success more than once to talk to the Grayson woman," Dorothy said as they left the Chestertons after lunch, "but I assume you're ready to try again."

"I am," Hale admitted.

"This time, ride with me there on my motorcycle."

"You're not going along!"

"You don't have to shout." Dorothy blinked her clear blue eyes and lit a cigarette. Enoch somehow looked even more handsome when he was trying to assert himself. "You aren't afraid of motorcycles, are you?"

"Don't be ridiculous. Of course not. I'm just trying to restore the natural order of the universe. I'm a journalist. I work alone."

"But I'm a copywriter. We work together." *Touché!* Disappointingly, the cleverness of her retort seemed lost on Enoch.

"Then get back to your office and work together with Reggie Smythe-Dickey!" he snapped.

She would—if only she could get Hale to go along and help her find out what Reggie was up to, and who he was. But that wasn't going to happen until Hale followed every other bread crumb first. Right now, inspired by the typically paradoxical musings of G.K. Chesterton, that meant talking to Lydia Grayson.

Dorothy, always more interested in winning the argument than in winning points, tried another tack. "Miss Grayson is probably avoiding you, Enoch. I'm sure she would be much more inclined to talk to one of her own sex." Dorothy was sure of no such thing, but it sounded good.

To Enoch's credit, he didn't give an automatic response. He stopped walking and looked at Dorothy. For a moment her soul felt quite naked. Her face got warm. Finally, he sighed. "They lived together above the Fitzroy Tavern. It's in—"

"Fitzrovia," Dorothy finished. "I know it well."

"I'm not surprised."

Enoch sat behind her on the Douglas 350, his manly arms around her waist, as they rode toward central London later that afternoon. With an effort of will, she concentrated on the road. But she found herself regretting that it was such a short trip.

The Fitzroy Tavern was located at 16 Charlotte Street, at the corner of Charlotte and Windmill Streets. Fitzrovia, the surrounding neighborhood to which the pub gave its name, was an artistic and Bohemian district made up of small, irregularly shaped streets. It wasn't as well off as the Bloomsbury area near her apartment, with its famous Bloomsbury Group of writers. Middle and lower classes mixed easily in the neighborhood. Dorothy had seen the playwright Shaw and the novelist Virginia Woolf walking those streets. Radical socialists liked to have a pint and save the world at the Fitzroy or at nearby Wheatsheaf's, both within a stone's throw of union offices and a Communist Party hall. Dorothy utterly rejected socialist theories as being based on a false understanding of human nature. But sometimes she liked to sit and watch the radicals with all the fascination of a patron at a zoo.

She would never know whether Lydia Grayson peeked out the window and saw that it was a woman calling or just happened to be home this time, but the previously elusive woman opened the door and agreed to speak with them about Langdale Pike.

"It can't hurt now," she said to Dorothy's puzzlement.

She led them into a modest apartment above the tavern, neat but small and sparsely furnished.

With a strong jawline and high cheekbones, Lydia Grayson was a handsome woman even though she made no attempt to enhance her looks. Her long sandy hair, piled carelessly on top of her head, was streaked with gray and she wore no face powder. Dorothy guessed her to be in her mid-forties, quite a bit younger than Pike had been. She was tall for a woman, about Dorothy's height, so that Dorothy found herself looking straight into a set of frank amber eyes. Her lean frame was conventionally clothed in a tight-waisted long blue skirt that ended a few inches above the ankle, a white blouse with fall-down collar, and a soft, black cardigan sweater. She looked the part of a lower middle-class worker more than a kept woman.

"Pike mentioned you to me a few times," Enoch told her. "He referred to you as his sister. But I've been told that you were . . . that you and he . . ."

Poor Enoch. He really was a kind man, Dorothy thought, afraid to embarrass Miss Grayson. The object of his concern put paid to that rather quickly.

"Yes, we were lovers," she said, possibly with a deliberate effort to shock. Was Dorothy imagining it or did she stand up straighter. "We've lived here together for ten years. I supported him in his work and he supported me in mine. Yes, Mr. Hale. I work. I write for various socialist publications under the sexless name of L.B. Grayson. Living together, sharing expenses and our bodies, was satisfactory for both of us. We found the bourgeois notion of marriage totally unnecessary. It couldn't give us anything we didn't already have."

Dorothy wondered if Miss Grayson would still feel that way when she realized that she had no standing under British law, none of the rights that a widow would have. Living as a wife without the legal benefits of a spouse seemed foolishly naïve to Dorothy. She realized that love might make a fool of her as well some day, but only in her own way.

"Langdale was quite sure, however, that the members of Arthur's and the other hypocrites from whom he made his bread and butter would be scandalized," Miss Grayson went on. "So he joined them in their hypocrisy by adopting the charade that we were siblings."

"Did that upset you?" Enoch asked. Was the direction of his thoughts really that obvious, Dorothy wondered, or did it just seem so to her because she knew why he was asking? Of course he wondered whether years of frustration with Pike had spilled out into poisoned tea.

"By no means," Miss Grayson said. "It was a strategic decision that allowed him to continue working in the heart of darkness."

"I don't get your meaning," Dorothy said as Enoch wrote in his Moleskin notebook.

Miss Grayson sat down in a chair, back straight, and crossed her legs. Ironically, she looked like royalty. She didn't invite her visitors to sit, although there was a love seat right across from her. "Langdale's real work was to gut the social order from within, sticking his knife into the capitalists, the aristocracy, and the so-called 'nobility' one at a time. I quite enjoyed watching."

The woman also enjoyed crowing for an audience, Dorothy realized. "So Pike was a socialist, too?"

"In theory we are communists, Miss Sayers, but the Russians seem to be giving that a bad name."

As a woman, Dorothy would never be allowed entrance into Arthur's, which bothered her not at all. She was rather sure, however, that the egalitarian ideals of Marx and Engels were not much on display there. She wondered fleetingly whether Pike was having his woman on.

Enoch looked around. "These are pleasant enough rooms, Miss Grayson, but not what I would have expected of a man who was said to have made a four-figure income two decades ago."

"We chose not to live like the parasites, Mr. Hale. We've used that dirty money to fund certain journals that promote our beliefs."

So that was how Pike had wooed and won the attractive revolutionary—by financing the armchair revolutionists. "Would those be the socialist publications that you write for?" Dorothy asked.

Favoring her with a venomous look, Lydia Grayson stood up. "Are you finished, now?"

"Not quite," Enoch said. "I haven't asked you the most important question. Who do you think might have wanted to kill Pike?"

"I couldn't tell you that. I would face an action for slander!"

Dorothy pounced. "So you have ideas, then!"

Lydia Grayson smiled viciously. "Some women do, you know."

A feminist herself, Dorothy felt the rebuke like a fist in the face.

"You don't have to worry about a lawsuit," Enoch said, "because I won't quote you in a story. I'm just looking for leads. Just tell me what you told Scotland Yard."

"They didn't ask my opinion. Since you did, I'll tell you what I think." Going over it in her mind later, Dorothy became convinced that Pike's mistress had just been playing coy about not sharing her suspicions. In reality, she could barely wait. If they had left at that point she probably would have run after them shouting names. "Scotland Yard should take a hard look at some of the men he ruined with his paragraphs."

Dorothy looked at Enoch. That was it? Even Dorothy, whose reading habits leaned more toward *The Times* and *The Morning Telegraph* than the gossip press, knew enough about Pike's career to have made the same suggestion. But Miss Grayson went on. She singled out four men as particularly worthy of measuring for the hangman's noose:

Horatio Bottomley, the journalist and former M.P., was exposed as a swindler in part through Pike's efforts. His bogus "John Bull Victory Bond Club," designed to prey on the sympathy of patriots, had gone down just the year before, in 1921. In May he had been convicted of fraudulent conversion of investors' funds. In addition to being sentenced to seven years' imprisonment, he was expelled from Parliament.

Lord Randolph Pringle lost his position as chairman of Lloyds Bank after Pike reported on his penchant for gambling at after-hours clubs and at race tracks.

Sir James Forrester's engagement to the beautiful daughter of Lord Halsey, the famous horse breeder, was called off after a report of his late-night sporting in the company of twin "ladies" of dubious reputation.

Basil Westlake's expected appointment as Minister of Justice in the last government was derailed by Pike's hints that he was a war profiteer. As a major in the Great War he had handled a wide variety of contracts for material. Major Westlake seemed to have lived well beyond his salary as an army officer. Some of the more important contracts for supplies appeared to be filled with substandard equipment. Nothing was proven, however, and the investigation stopped when his name was withdrawn from consideration for the cabinet post.

"Those were all very public men, and each had a very public fall from grace as a result of Langdale's efforts," Miss Grayson said. "Revenge is a powerful motive, I'm sure you'll agree."

Enoch did agree, if Dorothy read his face correctly.

"The notion is certainly something to work with," he said.

THIRTEEN
Process of Elimination

Lost in the gloom of uninspired research.
– William Wordsworth, *The Excursion*

"You really meant it, didn't you, about treating those four men as suspects?" Dorothy asked as they left.

"That's as good a plan as any."

"I think Grayson was just trying to draw suspicion away from herself."

Hale, in the act of climbing onto the Douglas 350 behind Dorothy, stopped and stared. What was this, some kind of female jealousy thing? "She seemed to have been getting everything she wanted out of him. Why kill him?"

"We have no confirmation for anything she said," Dorothy pointed out. "We only have her word that the relationship was so satisfactory, and not the slightest idea what her word is worth. Perhaps he was really a follower of Mussolini, and not a socialist, for example. Or maybe she didn't actually approve of what he was doing. Or maybe he found a new lover."

"Miss Grayson could never get into Arthur's to drug the tea without being noticed. There are too few women working there. And what about your suspicions of Smythe-Dickey?"

"Maybe he and Grayson did it together."

"A conspiracy?" Hale didn't even try to keep the amusement out of his voice.

"Why not? The works of Phillips Oppenheim are full of them."

"But this isn't a spy story."

Dorothy's eyes widened. "Maybe that's just what it is—some kind of spy business!"

"You really are a very creative woman, Dorothy." Hale finished getting onto her motorcycle. "After you drop me off you should put all that talent to work doing what you're paid to do. Smythe-Dickey must be looking all over for you."

Dorothy gunned the motor and peeled away from the curb before Hale's foot was quite off the ground.

When she stopped in front of the Central Press Syndicate offices, clearly in no happy mood, Hale's body was still vibrating from the journey. Dorothy wasn't a bad driver, though, he had to admit. A few weeks earlier he'd accepted a lift from T.E. Lawrence after an interview about the Colonel's new book, *The Seven Pillars of Wisdom*. Lawrence should stick to riding camels. The way he drove a motorcycle, he was going to get himself killed someday.

Hale got off the vehicle. *Maybe this is a mistake*, he thought. Maybe he shouldn't be so quick to send Dorothy on her way. She could be helpful. He might never have gotten in to see Lydia Grayson without her.

"Dorothy," he started to say. But the sound of the engine cut him off. Within seconds he was choking on the smoke coming out of the exhaust pipe of her motorcycle.

It was late afternoon. Ned Malone sat in the nearly deserted CPS newsroom banging on a typewriter.

"What are you working on, Ned?" Hale asked.

"Shhh." Malone looked around guiltily. "It's another Challenger adventure. It's so amazing that . . . Oh, what's the use? Nobody will ever believe it. Even I don't believe it, and I was there." He tore the paper out of the typewriter, crumpled it into a ball, and tossed it in a wastebasket.

Hale tried to pretend he wasn't consumed with curiosity about the discarded page. "I'm glad you're here, Ned. Maybe you can help me figure out what to do next." As quickly as he could, he summarized his interviews with G.K. Chesterton and Lydia Grayson. The tale was impossible to tell without alluding to the role of Dorothy L. Sayers.

"You sound a bit taken with this Sayers girl," Malone said when he'd finished.

"What? Don't be silly. You've met Sadie. I'd marry her in a minute, if I could."

"Of course you would, old man! The real question is whether you would marry Lady Sarah Bridgewater . . . if you could."

This was cutting a bit too close to the bone for Hale. He changed the subject. "Didn't you cover the downfall of Horatio Bottomley back when you were with *The Daily Gazette*?"

"I covered the trial," Malone corrected. "Miss Grayson was right when she told you that Pike was the one who gave the first hint there was something bent about his investment scheme. But not everybody liked him even before that. Bernard Shaw went to one of his war rallies and was typically devastating in his account of it. I think I still remember part of it word for word: 'It is exactly what I expected, the man gets his popularity by telling people with a sufficient bombast just what they think themselves and therefore want to hear.'"

Hale chuckled. "Well, nobody could ever accuse Shaw of telling people what they want to hear—just the bombast part. As someone who's seen Bottomley close up, what do you think of him as a suspect for Pike's murder?"

"I think the role would fit him like a glove if he weren't safely behind bars in Maidstone Prison. He's already started his sentence."

Miss Grayson had mentioned three other men. And Hale still wondered about the nebulous Harrison Scott. He asked Malone if any of the names was familiar to him.

"Lord Pringle blew his brains out in front of a crowd at Ascot Racecourse the day he was dismissed from Lloyds," Malone said.

"How the devil did you remember that?"

"I had a longshot that came in that day. It paid twelve to one."

Malone also recalled the names of Westlake and Forrester from the scandals surrounding them, but he didn't know what had happened to them. He'd never heard of Scott. "Let's check the morgue," he said.

Trosley, the librarian, had gone for the day. But with Malone's help it took only a few minutes to look up the three names in the Central Press Syndicate files, which included clippings from all the major British and European newspapers.

They found one small story on Westlake. He'd been given a minor post in Siam after his disappointment in not getting the ministry position. Not so bad, Hale thought. At least he still had whatever brains he started out with. Siam was a long way from Arthur's. Scratch him as a suspect.

But what if Westlake or Bottomley, or even both of them, had paid someone to poison Pike? Could it have been a conspiracy of people ruined by Pike to seek revenge, to kill off a mutual enemy? Hale shook his head. He was starting to think like Dorothy—and E. Phillips Oppenheim. He needed to concentrate on the probable first.

Harrison Scott apparently had never done anything newsworthy, or even gossip-worthy. None of the thousands of files in the CPS morgue had his name on it.

On the other hand, Sir James Forrester, his plans to marry into a family even wealthier than his own dashed, still cut quite a figure on the local social scene. Clip after clip from the London papers showed him at pubs and nightclubs about town. One of the stories, a fluffy piece by Howell of *The Times* about a charity ball that Sir James chaired, indicated that he began most of his free evenings at the legendary Cheshire Cheese Pub. The face that looked out at Hale from the photo accompanying the story—thin, with sensuous lips curled into a smirk under a droopy mustache—looked familiar to Hale.

"I think I've seen him at the Cheshire Cheese," Hale said. He consulted his watch. "It's just on six o'clock. I think I'll stop round there for a spot of dinner."

At about the same time, Dorothy Sayers was back on Charlotte Street in Fitzrovia. She hadn't mentioned to Hale that it wasn't far from her flat at 24 Great James Street. It was also the street where Mavis Pierce lived and pretended to paint, just a few houses down from the Fitzroy Tavern. Mavis hadn't been one of Dorothy's friends who called themselves the Mutual Admiration Society at Oxford, but they'd gotten along reasonably well. What could be more natural than that a Somerville graduate should drop by and see her old classmate?

"Dorothy? Is it really you?" Standing in the doorway of her flat, Mavis squealed like the schoolgirl she had once been.

"None other, old girl! I was having a pint at the Fitzroy and I thought to myself, 'Doesn't Mavis Pierce live around here somewhere, hobnobbing with that Bloomsbury Group and all those radicals?'"

"Well, you're the same old Dorothy, exaggerating everything. Come on in."

After five minutes of tea and chat, Dorothy casually said, "You probably know a friend of mine who lives above the Fitzroy—Lydia Grayson."

"Oh, yes, I certainly do."

"I rather thought you might. Tell me, Mavis . . ."

The Cheshire Cheese Pub was just a couple of blocks away from Hale's office. The venerable public house at 145 Fleet Street, on Wine Office Court, had been a favorite hangout of the literary and newspaper crowds for four hundred years. Dr. Samuel Johnson and Charles Dickens had been at home there. In the present day politicians like Churchill and poets like W.B. Yeats were likely to find themselves elbow-to-elbow drinking at the Cheshire Cheese. Hale's newspaper friends could grab a pint and a meal there any hour of the day or night, and often did.

Hale himself spent enough time there that the irascible Polly greeted him by name, followed by an unprintable epithet, when he ducked into the pub from the narrow alley. No one seemed to know whether the foul-mouthed parrot had picked up her salty vocabulary from sailors (one of whom had mailed the bird to the pub in a cigar box) or journalists.

The gloom of the place was part of its charm, along with the interior wood paneling and the vaulted cellars from a thirteenth-century Carmelite monastery that had once occupied the site. Thirty or forty years ago there had been a brothel upstairs.

Hale made his way from one room to the next until, just on the verge of giving up, he spotted Forrester hoisting a whiskey at one of the bars. The man was a couple of inches taller than Hale and lean, with an air of Byronic dissipation. Hale estimated his age in the mid-thirties. For some unfathomable reason, he put Hale in mind of a vampire. Hale casually worked his way toward the bar. Within a few minutes he was standing next to his target. He lit a panatela and ordered a Fuller's London Porter.

Now what? Hale finally decided on the naïve Yank approach. "Aren't you Sir James Forrester?"

The baronet turned and gave Hale a searching look. "Do I know you?"

"Not really. We were introduced once."

"I'm sorry, I don't recall. When was that?"

"Oh, it's been a few months. Lady Somebody or Other brought us together at that ball for the London Arts Council. We only chatted briefly. I'm Enoch Hale."

Forrester nodded. "Of course." He managed a social smile that did not reach his cold eyes, but made no effort to offer his hand.

"I certainly admire your work with the Arts Council. I'm something of a writer myself, in a minor way. I'm a journalist. Fascinating business. Wake up in the morning and you never know what you're going to be writing about that day. Lately I've been covering the murder of Langdale Pike."

Forrester's smile faded. "Pike!"

Hale sipped the porter. "Did you know him?"

"Too bloody well." Forrester drank the last of his whiskey and set the glass down on the bar with a thud. "You journalist johnnies never think about how what you write can hurt a man."

Hale tried to look offended. "Well, Pike and I didn't exactly work the same side of the street, so to speak. He wrote for the trash papers. Nobody ever really reads those things, do they?"

Forrester's expression turned rueful. "Apparently they do. Somehow Pike found out about a little dalliance I had going with a couple of sisters. It was nothing serious, you understand. They weren't the sort of girls one would *marry*. It was just, you know, fun. But Pike wrote about it. And do you know what happened?"

Your fiancée gave you the old heave-ho. "I haven't the foggiest."

"My club asked me to resign."

Hale could hardly believe his ears. That's what Forrester was most upset about? "Your club?"

"Too bloody right." He signaled the barman for another whiskey. "Arthur's. I'd been a member for almost ten years. Pike was a member, too. He was there every day, buying and selling gossip. Mr. Bloody Member of Parliament Standish didn't mind that, but he made me resign just for having a bit of sport with a couple of willing lasses. Standish! His skirts aren't so bloody clean, are they? He should have thrown himself out of the club!"

This sounded promising. "What do you mean?"

The barman started to set a whiskey in front of Forrester, but the baronet snatched it almost before it touched the bar. "Well, where did he get all his money? And what are those private meetings he has behind closed doors at Arthur's?"

Hale felt a sting of disappointment. Forrester was clearly grasping at straws in his near-drunken anger. Standish came from a wealthy family.

"Who do you think killed Pike?" Hale asked.

"I couldn't even guess," Forrester said. He held up his whiskey glass in toasting gesture. "But here's to him!"

FOURTEEN
The 43

A gay nightlife has the effect on looks and complexion of
a long spell of sickness.
> – Jean Paul Richter, *Hesperus*

Forrester seemed almost as angry with Standish as
with Pike, Hale thought. Or did he just want Hale to think
that? As a former member of Arthur's, he would know
Pike's routine with the tea. He might also know which
waiter he could hire to poison it. Sir James Forrester stayed
on the suspect list.

And so did Harrison Scott. The difficulty in finding
out anything about him was highly suspect. How could a
man be a member of a social club like Arthur's and never
get his name in a newspaper?

Hale needed to talk to someone who knew things
that didn't appear in newspapers—someone like Langdale
Pike, in fact. Since that wasn't an option, where else could
Hale go? He immediately thought of Patrick Balfour, who
signed his column in *The Sketch* as "Mr. Gossip."

In a few hours, Hale knew, Balfour would be
collecting gossip at the after-hours nightclub called The 43.
Hale could catch up to him there. The famous, or infamous,

unlicensed club was owned by an Irish woman named Mrs. Meyrick. Hale had heard somewhere that she had six children and was divorced from a doctor who ran an asylum in Brighton for shellshock victims from the Great War. She encouraged gossip columnists to visit her establishment as a way of promoting the business. Balfour, among others, wrote about all the up-and-comers, politicians, actors, and so forth who frequented The 43.

The 43 didn't even open until midnight. To kill time until then, Hale at first thought of writing Sadie a letter. Instead, he stopped by J&E Bumpus, Booksellers, on Oxford Street. It took him about twenty minutes of searching the store to find what he was looking for. It was a slim brown volume in limp leather called *Op. I.*—Dorothy L. Sayers's first book of poetry. Hale wasn't sure whether calling it "first work" in Latin was condemnably presumptuous or admirably ambitious. Since there had been a second work, he leaned toward the latter interpretation.

Hale had never bought a book of poetry until now, but he found himself intensely curious as to what sort of poems Dorothy would write. Back at his flat, he paged through the book, looking for something to catch his non-poetical eye. He counted fourteen poems, some of them rather long, with themes drawing on mythology, Arthurian legend, Sacred Scripture, and the writer's own experiences of love and college days at Oxford. They actually had rhythm and rhyme. Eliot probably would have been appalled at this conventionality, but Hale liked his poetry to be, well, poetic.

The first poem, after the dedication and even before the table of contents, seemed a rather bold announcement of the author's intentions:

I WILL build up my house from the stark foundations,
If God will give me time enough,
And search unwearying over the seas and nations
For stones or better stuff.

Though here be only the mortar and rough-hewn
granite,
I will lay on and not desist
Till it stand and shine as I dreamed it when I began it,
Emerald, amethyst.

Hale wasn't sure whether Pound, or Yeats, or any of
Tom Eliot's other poet pals would rate Dorothy's poems as
precious gems, but at least he could understand them. Some
of them, in fact, seemed all too clear, like "Hymn in
Contemplation of a Sudden Suicide" and "Epitaph for a
Young Musician." Reading some of the poems with great
attention, and skimming through others, he came to the end
in a few hours. The last poem was his favorite of the bunch.
It was called "Last Morning in Oxford" and dated June
23rd, 1915:

I DO not think that very much was said
Of solemn requiem for the good years dead.

Like Homer, with no thunderous rhapsody,
I closed the volume of my Odyssey.

The thing that I remember most of all
Is the white hemlock by the garden wall.

Hale didn't feel that kind of sweet nostalgia for
Yale, but he wished he did. He closed the book with a sigh
and headed for Soho.

Just as the Volstead Act in the United States had created a boom in the illegal booze industry for the likes of William McCoy, "Big Bill" Dwyer, and their rum running friends, the Defense of the Realm Act in Great Britain had led to the proliferation of unlicensed after-hours nightclubs. The original act required nightclubs to close at 9 P.M. The after-hours clubs sprang up to meet the demands of visiting American and Canadian officers, as well as the drinking British. After the War this was liberalized to 11 P.M., or midnight if food was served. The unlicensed competition to the legal nightclubs just pushed back their hours and imported American jazz bands for entertainment.

The43 took its name from its location at 43 Gerrard Street in Soho, the premier entertainment area of London. A blue plaque on the building stated that the poet John Dryden had lived there in 1697. That sounded very classy, but Hale had heard that Gerrard Street had the third largest number of prostitutes of any street in London. He had no personal knowledge of that, but he had been to The 43 a few times. It wasn't a place he would have taken Sadie, although she would have enjoyed it just to prove herself thoroughly modern. Its popularity among the "Bright Young Things" was attributable entirely to its disrespectability.

Mrs. Meyrick sat behind the cash desk of her office on the ground floor of the dingy little joint. She was not well dressed, but she had something of a motherly appearance. Well groomed and with charming manners, she was small, middle aged, with bow legs and untidy brown hair. She could not have looked more out of place in a club that catered to the evening dress set. Like the dragon at the gate, she decided who did and did not get in. University students, guardsmen, and the aristocracy always made it through. With an eye toward publicity, she also liked journalists.

"Always good to see you, Mr. Hale," she rasped, her rough voice equal parts Irish and Irish whiskey. She must have had a good memory, probably cultivated with care. Hale didn't go there that often.

"It's always good to be seen by you, you beautiful creature." The Irish had no corner on blarney. Mrs. Meyrick giggled. "How many coppers do you bribe to keep this place open?"

"Ah, now, Mr. H, ask me no questions and I'll tell you no lies."

Hale paid the ten-shilling fee for non-members and was admitted. Although there was a lounge with a bar on the first floor, Hale quickly made his way down to the basement. That's where the action was. The rectangular room, three times longer than it was wide, had a small dance floor with wooden chairs and tables clustered around it. The band, which was now on break, included a piano, a banjo, drums, a trumpet and a saxophone.

On this Friday night, Hale estimated the attendance at more than ninety representatives of the smart set. Capacity was eighty. Some of the couples were made up of two men or two women. Mrs. Meyrick didn't care about that, as long as they didn't dance together. She employed more than two dozen well-paid dance hostesses, known as "Merry Maids," who got paid a commission on sales of Champagne, which went for three times the going rate.

But Hale wasn't there for dancing or bubbly. He looked around the crowded room for Balfour. Italian waiters, illegal immigrants, bustled around. Just a few weeks before, Balfour had reported that a drunken patron mistook Rudolph Valentino for one of the waiters. Well, the actor was Italian by birth.

"Hale, old chap, what are you doing here?" said a soft voice.

Hale whirled around to see Aloysius Bone, his curly head barely coming up to Hale's shoulder. Their encounter the day before had not been particularly pleasant, but Bone acted as if they were old pals.

"Just looking for a friend," Hale said.

"Mr. Gossip?"

"What makes you say that?"

"Pike is dead. You need a source of information for the social gossip you used to get from him. Balfour has a reputation in that line, and Balfour is almost as closely associated with The 43 as Pike was Arthur's. It's elementary, really, as somebody once said."

Hale was impressed despite himself. He might almost respect Bone if he didn't despise him.

"So where is he?"

Bone shrugged his slight shoulders. "Everybody needs a night off now and then. Perhaps I could be of assistance."

"I doubt it." Bone's attempts to build his career on the sleazy side of journalism were almost pathetic. Still . . . it couldn't hurt to ask. "I'm trying to find out something about a member of Arthur's called Harrison Scott."

Bone's dark skin paled. "I've never heard of him."

Hale had seen this kind of reaction before—from Pike himself a couple of years before when Hale had asked him about a man known to Hale only as "M." It turned out that the "M" was for "Mycroft," and the man was head of His Majesty's Secret Service as well as being Sherlock Holmes's older brother. Hale would have liked to have forgotten the entire episode, if only he could.

"You've heard of Scott, all right. Spill. What do you know? Who is he? And why don't you want to talk about him?"

Bone looked around the dance hall as if checking for eavesdroppers. "Such men are dangerous, you know."

"So am I." Hale tried to look menacing. From the look on Bone's face, he thought he succeeded. "Look, Aloysius, you're safer talking here than at a midnight rendezvous. We're just two old friends who happened to run into each other during a night on the town. Believe me, every man here has one thing on his mind, and it's not you."

"I should have known better than to speak to you." Bone sighed. "All right, then. We'd better sit down. As it happens I learned quite a bit about Mr. Scott before I discovered that it would be safer not to learn any more."

They found a table that was just being evacuated by two other men.

Bone lit a cigarette. His hands shook slightly. "Despite his last name, Scott is Welsh by birth, English by upbringing. His father is an industrialist, his mother an heiress. He's a director of one of his father's companies, what you Americans would call a vice-president, and travels around the world a lot on business. He speaks fluent Italian, French, and Russian. He's also an excellent horseman and a fair shot."

"A playboy?"

"Not exactly, old chap. After attending the best public schools and graduating from Sandhurst, he served with the Welsh regiment at Suvla Bay in the Dardanelles as a captain. He was wounded there and taken prisoner by German advisors to the Turks. Scott got lucky on that—the Turks would have shot him like they did all prisoners. But the Germans took him back to the Fatherland and put him in a POW camp for officers at Strasland. He and two others escaped and made their way by boat to Sweden. When he finally got back to England he found out he'd received the VC for action in Suvla."

Bone paused.

"And?" Hale prodded.

"That's it. That's what I know."

"The man's led an exemplary life. Did you give up on him because there's no gossip for you to write about?"

"No, that wasn't it. Within twenty-four hours after I started asking around about Scott I got a visit from two gentlemen that even you wouldn't want to meet in a dark alley. They asked me very politely to back off. Since they asked so nicely—and since I hate the sight of blood, especially my own—I did what they asked. Now, why don't you do both of us a favor and forget everything I just told you?"

Hale didn't respond. He was thinking. Lots of folks didn't like being fodder for the gossip columns, and he didn't blame them. But why would a respectable businessman bother to send two thugs to put a lid on Aloysius Bone? That's the kind of thing that gangsters were doing back home in the States.

All of a sudden, the penny dropped.

Gangsters, Prohibition, rum running.

Hale knew just the sort of businessmen who often used strong-arm tactics. He'd written several stories about their ilk.

FIFTEEN
The Diogenes Club

Men still have to be governed by deception.
— G.C. Lichtenberg, *Reflections*

Could it really be that Scott had something to do with rum running, and that Pike had to be silenced because he found out about it? Hale couldn't see why not. He intended to talk it through with Rathbone on Saturday morning, but Tweedledee and Tweedledum intervened.

That's how he always thought of the two matching bulldog-like men who showed up at his door that morning as he was ready to go to his office. He'd never learned their real names, if they had any. M had only referred to them as his "associates" when they had first met two years ago. But to him they were like the two characters from *Alice*, which happened to be one of Dorothy Sayers's favorite and most often-quoted books.

"Not again," he muttered to himself.

"Good morning, Mr. Hale," said Tweedledee.

"Not any more. I suppose we're going for a ride again?"

"If you don't mind." The agent gave a half-smile, not even bothering to show his gun. That did nothing to reassure Hale. He knew what M and his "associates" were capable of, and it wasn't pleasant.

The silent ride to the Diogenes Club, the eccentric private club in Pall Mall from whence the aged Mycroft Holmes presided over His Majesty's Secret Service, wasn't a long one. Hale barely had time to speculate on how he had gotten in the old man's way this time.

Behind the Greek columns of the Diogenes Club the most unclubable men in the British Empire sat in overstuffed chairs reading their newspapers, forbidden by club rules from paying the slightest attention to each other. Tweedledum and Tweedledee swept Hale up a marble staircase and into the Strangers Room, the only room in which members of the Diogenes Club and their guests were allowed to converse.

It appeared to be empty except for one man sitting in a leather wingback chair. He smiled in satisfaction at their entrance. "Welcome back, Mr. Hale."

"The pleasure is all yours, Mycroft."

Hale put a slight emphasis on the name. Two years earlier, in this very room, the old man had introduced himself as M. The intervening time had not been kind to Mycroft Holmes, a man well into his seventies. Though still rotund, he seemed to be dwindling in size all around, like a melting snowman. His face sagged a bit, but the watery eyes sunken within still looked sharp.

M clucked. "My, my, you do seem testy this morning. Perhaps if you fired that clumsy servant girl you would start your days in a better mood."

The Holmes brothers indulged in this parlor trick of telling people about themselves all the time. Hale made up his mind not to be distracted by it.

"What is it this time?" he asked. "Why did you have your goons bring me here?"

The two agents looked so crestfallen at Hale's characterization of them that he almost apologized.

"Right down to business, eh?" M said. "How very American of you. Very well. I understand you've been making certain inquiries. I want to introduce you to someone who can help you. I warn you, however, that from this point forward everything that happens in this room is under the protection of the Official Secrets Act. If you print one word of it, I'll have you arrested."

M had made the threat before, and Hale knew that it wasn't an idle one. "I get the picture."

The old man made a motion and one of the agents—the one Hale thought of as Tweedledum—opened a side door, not the one through which Hale had entered. A man with military-style bearing and mustache came into the room. He had dark brown hair and matching eyes, lean but powerfully built. Hale put his age at just under thirty.

"Harrison Scott," the newcomer announced, putting out his hand to Hale. Numbly, Hale shook it.

"Everything that you have likely learned about Captain Scott's military service and his business career are true," M said. "However, there is a secret history as well. Because of Mr. Scott's impressive language skills, I sent him back to Sweden to gather information on the Bolsheviks from escaping White Russians and to help other men escape German POW camps. After the War, he remained on with us in His Majesty's Secret Service. His business activities are a convenient cover for his extensive travels."

"And His Majesty doesn't mind if I make a pound or two for the family firm on the side," Scott said, straightening the cuff of his Savile Row suit coat.

He looked like an effete toff, but Hale wasn't fooled by that. M's men were tough, and they'd practically been given a license to kill. *Yes, to kill.* The thought hit Hale like a bullet in the head.

"You killed Pike, didn't you?"

Scott gaped.

"Don't be ridiculous," M snapped. "Pike was ours, too."

"Pike? An agent?" Hale felt disoriented, out of focus. This was all coming at him too fast.

"Not an agent, per se, but a key informant," Scott said. "He had been for years. In return, we passed him information for his paragraphs. Of course, it was always information that we wanted to see printed, and sometimes it was even true. Most recently, Pike was supplying me with intelligence on a group of White Russians who are plotting to go back into Russia."

"That's a good thing, right?"

"No, that's a bad thing. They don't know it, but their activities could upset secret trade negotiations between His Majesty's Government and the new Soviet Union." The look Hale gave must have asked the next question. "After so long and devastating a war, neither we nor our allies are going to be embroiled in a useless affair in Russia. So I need to . . . get them off track."

With a neatly aimed bullet, maybe?

M turned over a flipper of a hand. "So you see, Mr. Hale, it could very well be that whoever killed Pike was acting against British interests. That's where we come in, and that's why we should very much like to know what you have found out in your investigation."

"I wouldn't call it an investigation," Hale said. "I'm a reporter. I've been asking questions."

"And hardly more subtle about it than the good Watson," came a familiar voice.

A tall figure stirred out of his place of concealment in an overstuffed chair facing a window. "However, sometimes the bull in the china shop manages to do more than break things."

"Holmes!"

Hale rushed over and pumped the detective's hand. "My word, it's good to see you again." The others in the room would never have guessed that an enraged Hale had once slammed the door of Holmes's Sussex cottage so hard upon leaving that the windows had rattled.

Though older now than he was portrayed in the magazine drawings that had made his face familiar throughout the world, Sherlock Holmes retained the hawk-like nose and piercing gray eyes that missed nothing.

"I'm sorry that you have lost the company of the charming Miss Briggs," he said, "but I see that you have not wanted for female companionship."

"She's not—" Hale stopped. "How did you know…" "Oh, really, Hale." M sighed. "Isn't one Watson enough for Sherlock? If you intend to keep your dalliances secret, then don't be so careful about shaving and applying scent, especially after the Press has so widely reported Lord Sedgewood's departure for Egypt with his beautiful daughter in tow."

Female companionship? A dalliance? Could that really be why he spent an extra five minutes grooming himself this morning? Hale shook off the preposterous thought.

"I'm not having a dalliance," Hale said, for the record. "The only woman I've been seeing lately is an advertising copywriter who insisted on accompanying me on some interviews."

"Those interviews," Holmes said. "Tell us about them. No, wait. Start before that, my boy. Tell us about your aborted tea with Langdale Pike and go on from there, leaving out nothing."

As quickly and succinctly as possible, Hale did so.

Holmes interrupted when he got to the part about the attack that had deprived him of Pike's notebook. "Friend Wiggins was kind enough to tell me about that. I've asked my old comrade Shinwell Johnson to try to find out the name of your assailant."

Porky Shinwell! Why hadn't Hale thought of him? The bruiser, a secretly reformed criminal, had been a kind of double agent for years. Moving freely among his former colleagues in crime in a way that only a man with two prison terms in his past could do, he frequently acquired information of interest to the law. Since the retirement of Sherlock Holmes, his original client, he continued to provide this service to both private and public detectives who he was sure would not mention his betrayal in the wrong places.

"Fortunately, I remembered some of the names in the diary," Hale said. "Or maybe it wasn't fortunate. Maybe I've been chasing wild geese all week."

He tried to make his account as complete as possible, relating his conversations over the past few days with Churchill, Bone, Chesterton, and the *dramatis personae* at Benson's as well as what he considered his more important discussions with Standish, Miss Grayson, and Forrester.

The Holmes brothers, sitting now in adjacent chairs facing Hale, listened intently.

"I really must congratulate you," Sherlock Holmes said at the end. "It is true that you have done everything possible to alert the killer that you are on his trail, but I suppose he's astute enough to know that anyway."

Mycroft Holmes—who would always be "M" to Hale—snorted. "He also called attention to Scott here, one of my most important agents."

Scott tried to look modest at these words of praise from the powerful man who at times *was* the British Government. He failed miserably. For a secret agent, he wasn't much of an actor.

"Try to remember, Sherlock, that matters of State crucial to the empire are at issue here," the older brother added.

"I was never in danger of forgetting that," said Sherlock Holmes. "Nor can I forget that Langdale Pike was

for many years a source of reliable information to me
regarding social scandal, an arcane world about which I
knew little. His murder aroused my pique enough to
dislodge me once again from my comfortable surroundings
on the Downs."

Mycroft raised an eyebrow. "How unlike you,
Sherlock. Pique is an emotion."

It suddenly occurred to Hale that this was the first
time he'd ever seen the Holmes brothers together. Despite
the difference in weight, the family resemblance between
the two was as clear as the aquiline noses on their faces.
And so was the sibling rivalry. They were acting like two
little boys arguing over a pet tortoise.

"I'm sure my efforts were quite inadequate," Hale
said, raising his voice a little to reclaim center stage. "I never
claimed to be a detective. I'm just a journalist. May I ask
what the real sleuthhound has been up to?"

"Oh, I've been on the inside of the murder scene,
working at Arthur's. I saw you there talking to Standish."

"But I didn't see you."

"On the contrary, my dear Hale," said Sherlock
Holmes. "You saw, but you did not recognize. That's
because you weren't intended to."

"Excuse me." A stiff, palace guard sort with gray
hair bent over Mycroft Holmes and handed him a note.
Hale hadn't even heard the man enter. M thanked him,
unfolded the note, quickly read it, and folded it back up
again. He said nothing.

Hale ignored the sideshow. "So what did you find
out?" he asked Sherlock Holmes.

"Very little, save for the identity of the murderer."

"What! Who was it?"

"The waiter, of course. Timothy Flood."

An image of the handsome young man immediately
formed in Hale's mind—the thick blond hair, the wide blue
eyes, the deferential and perhaps rather scared manner.

Could it really be that after all of Hale's running around like Nick Carter or Sexton Blake the killer was the waiter who had served Pike the tea? How anti-climatic! From the point of view of opportunity he was the most obvious suspect, but Hale had never considered him seriously because he seemed to lack any possible motive.

"Why him?"

"I learned from my colleagues at Arthur's that he wasn't supposed to work on Tuesday—he traded days with another waiter, claiming that he needed Saturday off instead. And then he siphoned the hot water for Pike's tea himself, something usually done by the bus boys."

"I mean," said Hale, "why would Flood kill Pike?"

Sherlock Holmes sighed. "That's yet to be established. I was hoping that your inquiries would provide a clue, and perhaps they have. Something you said gave me just a glimmer of a possibility—enough to confront Flood with, at any rate."

"I'm afraid that will not be possible," M rumbled. He held up the folded note in his hand. "I have just been informed that Flood's body was found this morning at his home. It appears that he shot himself."

SIXTEEN
Corpse of a Killer

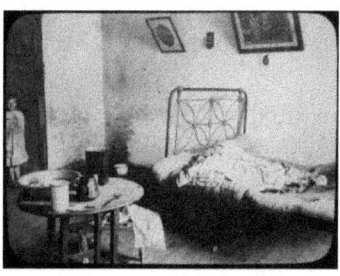

Simply to kill a man is not murder.
    – Thomas De Quincy, *On Suicide*

The Flood family home, where Timothy Flood had
died, was on Hoxton Road in Hoxton, in the East End. It
was a poor area full of boot and furniture factories, the
former single-family residences now broken up into cheap
flats. The Floods lived in the basement flat of a two-story
brick house. Hale and Holmes climbed four steps to the
front door, then down a stairwell into the basement.

Chief Inspector Wiggins and two other Scotland
Yard men were still there in the main room of the flat,
along with the body. Hale heard a woman crying behind a
closed door. The shooting apparently had happened while
she had been out with the other children last evening. She
had found the body this morning.

"It's a rum business and no mistake, Mr. Holmes."
Wiggins shook his head. "Flood supported his mother and
the other five children. The father died in a railroad
accident three years ago."

Young Timothy Flood lay on his back on the floor, his arms spread to the right and left. *He doesn't look so handsome now*, Hale thought. Near the right hand was a wet spot on the hardwood floor. A pistol, which Hale recognized as a Colt .45, lay about six feet from Flood's left foot.

"There's a single bullet hole in the heart with some scorching around the shirt front, as we would expect," Wiggins said. "I'm sure you've noticed, Mr. Holmes, that the hammer is back on the pistol to fire another shot."

"Indeed," muttered Holmes. But his eyes were already elsewhere, focused on a cheap table with a bottle of Jameson's Irish whiskey and a single glass along with brochures from the Cunard Line and ferry schedules for Dublin. "He left a note, sir." Wiggins handed it to Holmes. Hale peered over his shoulder. The message was brief and unadorned: *"Murder is a grave sin that I have committed. I cannot go on. Please forgive me. Timothy Flood."*

"His handwriting, I presume?" Holmes said.

Wiggins nodded. "It compares fairly to a sample his mother gave us. *'Gone to the store. Be back soon. Timothy.'* The writing is a little wobbly, not a perfect match, but he'd been drinking."

Holmes got down on his knees and smelled the wet spot on the floor. "Yes, it's the Jameson's." He stood back up and studied the brochures on the table. "It looks like he was planning a trip, not self-murder."

"You know that happens all the time—a man makes plans for the future right before he kills himself," Wiggins said. "It's no use looking for logic in suicides. In this case Flood must have been overcome by the horror of what he did, killing Mr. Pike."

"Flood may have killed Pike, but he didn't kill himself," Hale said.

Where did that come from?

"Go on," Holmes said in an encouraging tone.

Hale paused to wrap logic around his intuition. "Flood must have been involved with the IRA. They've been very active lately—you know they killed Field Marshal Wilson just two days ago. Maybe Pike caught wind of that in advance and he had to be killed to silence him. The ferry schedule on that table points to Flood's Dublin connection. And the Cunard brochures show how he was intending to flee the country."

"On a Cunard ship? An Irish waiter?" The chief inspector's voice was rich with skepticism.

"Cunard has more steerage berths than first class," Hale snapped back. "Flood was going to run away because he killed Pike. But the IRA got to him because they were afraid he'd talk when the heat got too much."

"And the suicide note?" Holmes asked.

Hale waved the implied objection away. "It doesn't say he was going to kill himself. It says 'I cannot go on.' Maybe he was writing to his superiors in the IRA saying he wanted out, and that's why they had to kill him."

"A very neat theory, I must say," Wiggins acknowledged. "Almost believable, even. Still—"

"My son had nothing to do with the IRA."

Every head in the room jerked toward the sound of the deep Irish voice. A sturdy woman stood in the open doorway of a bedroom, handsome but tired looking, with sandy hair and blue eyes. She was probably in her mid-forties. Hale could see a large crucifix on a wall of the room behind her.

"He was no murderer," she went on. "And he didn't kill himself, neither."

"I'm sorry, Mrs. Flood," said Sherlock Holmes. "I know this must be very difficult for you." He spoke kindly, the cold, unemotional reasoner nowhere in sight.

"A woman knows her own son than anyone else, faults and all. Timothy was a hard worker and such a comfort to me and the young ones since his poor father died." The widow looked down at her folded hands. "The Good Lord knows he was no angel—a bit of a scamp with the lasses, was Timothy—but there was no real harm in him."

Hale didn't know what to say to that, and he could see that Wiggins didn't either. The chief inspector was obviously quite taken by Mrs. Flood and seemed to accept her judgment of her son.

"Excuse me." A round-faced man in a Roman collar stood in the entrance to the flat. He instantly reminded Hale of Chesterton's Father Brown. "I came as soon as I heard about the boy, Mary." He sounded like a Yorkshire man.

"Oh, Father O'Connor." The widow threw her arms around the little priest and dissolved into tears.

Without a further word, Sherlock Holmes led Hale, Wiggins, and the rest of the Scotland Yard men out of the flat. Their work there was finished, and Father O'Connor's was just beginning.

It didn't occur to Hale until later that Holmes hadn't expressed an opinion about his explanation of the death of Timothy Flood.

SEVENTEEN
A Scandal Explained

There are no secrets better kept than the secrets
everybody guesses.
— George Bernard Shaw

Two days later, with *The Morning Telegraph* at his
elbow blaring the headline **WAITER'S SUICIDE ENDS
CASE**, Hale began writing to Sadie. He'd already sent her
one letter, in which he'd told her about Pike's murder. She
should find his epistles waiting for her when she arrived at
Shepherd's Hotel in Cairo. The writer in him hoped that
she would read them in order so as to preserve the
suspense.

> *Quite a letdown, Sadie! The murderer wasn't G.K.
> Chesterton, someone connected with Benson's, or Sir
> James Forrester. He was a young waiter who was
> probably upset that Pike had spoken to him sharply or
> something of the sort. We really don't know why he
> poisoned the tea. That's the only mystery remaining.*
> *I hope that you are finding more excitement among
> your mummies. I've heard nothing out of Egypt since . . .*

He stopped writing and threw his pen across the room. No, no, no! He just didn't believe his own story. Why would Timothy Flood, sole support of his mother and five siblings, take the risk of killing a man just to avenge some slight, and then do away with himself in the bargain? Wiggins may have fallen for that hook, line, and sinker, but Hale didn't. He still believed what he'd said at Flood's house, right in front of the body: The young man may have killed Pike—probably for desperately needed money—but he didn't kill himself. If it wasn't the IRA, it was somebody else who had paid him.

Why didn't Sherlock Holmes see . . .? And that's when Hale realized that he didn't know what Holmes thought. He'd told the detective everything he had done or thought in this case, but Holmes had told him and Wiggins very little in return.

What would Dorothy Sayers think of these developments? That was no help—she'd just say that Smythe-Dickey or Lydia Grayson was behind it all. And maybe she was right.

It was early evening as Hale set his unfinished letter to Sadie aside. With the murder of Langdale Pike neatly tied up—all too neatly, Hale felt certain—Rathbone had ordered him back to work on the rum running story. He'd spent the day on the docks with nothing to show for it. A lot of alcohol passed through the London Docks, and Hale felt sure that some of it was being diverted to the other side of the Atlantic. But nobody was talking. So that avenue appeared to be a dead-end, at least for now.

But if Hale could break open the Pike/Flood story again by establishing that somebody else was behind the murder of Pike and had also killed Flood, that would be a big "scoop," as they called it in the States.

If somebody hired Flood to kill Pike, the waiter must have been seen in that person's company at some

point. But by whom? Not by his mother—Flood would
have been careful that she didn't get a whiff of any
shenanigans that he was caught up in. His co-workers at
Arthur's, then.

Within minutes Hale was heading out the door,
bound for Clubland.

On his way to St. James's Street he passed the
Diogenes Club in Pall Mall. What did canny old Mycroft
Holmes think of the solution accepted by Scotland Yard? It
was useless to speculate. Hale didn't even know what
Sherlock Holmes thought, and they had worked together
rather closely at the end of the Hangman case.

"I'd like to see Mr. Blanton," he told the stout
gentleman at the door of Arthur's.

"Do you have an—"

"Give him this." Hale scribbled a few words on a
business card.

A few minutes later the steward was back. "Come
this way, please."

He led Hale to the bar. To his surprise, George
Standish lifted a flute of Champagne in his direction,
smiled, and swallowed about a third of it. "I'm surprised to
see you back, Mr. Hale."

"No more surprised than I am to see you."

"This is my club. I am chairman of the management
committee."

"Yes, of course. I know that. I meant that I asked to
see Mr. Blanton."

"Mr. Blanton and I agreed that it would be better if
you see me. Care for a drink?"

Hale ordered a Manhattan from a young barman
with very little hair on his head and a handlebar mustache
stolen from a melodrama villain.

"I'll be frank, Mr. Hale," Standish went on. "The
unfortunate suicide of Mr. Flood has brought more

unfavorable publicity to Arthur's in the short run. That couldn't be helped. But I had hoped it meant that we would finally be out of our unaccustomed place in the public eye because the murder of Langdale Pike was solved. And now you come calling again, a journalist. Pray tell what bee is in your bonnet this time?"

Hale sipped his Manhattan for courage. "I don't think the Pike case is over."

Standish made a question mark of his eyebrows. "I'm afraid I don't understand. How can it not be over? Flood killed Pike and then himself."

"That's a very convenient solution for somebody, but I don't buy it. I think somebody else paid or coerced Flood into poisoning Pike. I was hoping that Blanton or some of Flood's friends in the kitchen might have seen him in the company of whoever that was. Think of it, Mr. Standish. What possible reason would a waiter scarcely older than a boy have for killing Langdale Pike?"

With a look of disgust on his face, Standish downed half of his remaining bubbly in a gulp. "Sodomy," he muttered.

"What?" Hale couldn't believe he had heard right. He'd been around artists and writers enough to know that "the love that dare not speak its name" wasn't exactly rare, but what did that have to do with Flood?

"I was hoping to keep this quiet, but it appears that the only way I'll dissuade you from this fool's errand you're on is by telling you the whole sordid tale—or as much of it as I know. Timothy Flood was buggering one of our members. Oh, don't look so shocked. I told you the other day that one of our members was involved in sodomite activity. Why not with a waiter? It happens all the time, dash it."

"But Flood was a Catholic! Aren't they down on that sort of thing?" He could imagine Mrs. Flood launching into a whole new set of hysterics if she heard about this.

Hale didn't need the look on Standish's self-satisfied face to tell him how foolish his question sounded.

"Oscar Wilde was also Catholic, at the end."

"So is that why Flood killed himself, fear that his weakness would be exposed?" Hale asked.

"He killed Pike! That's why he killed himself, isn't it?"

But Dorothy Sayers's logic still held: There was no reason to kill Pike to hide a secret that he'd already shared with someone else, namely Standish. In that case, the M.P. would be a target as well.

"I don't suppose somebody's tried to kill you lately," Hale said.

"Not that I'm aware," Standish responded dryly.

Hale thought a moment. "Who was the other man, the member that Flood was involved with?"

"I wouldn't tell you if I knew, but I don't. Pike refused to share that particular piece of information, almost as if he were a gentleman."

That took Hale by surprise. "But when we talked about this before you said you hoped to solve the problem with a quiet resignation."

Standish nodded. "Yes, that's right. I expected to demand Flood's resignation. But after the murder, I thought it best to wait a few days because I was afraid that his departure would attract unwanted attention under the circumstances."

So maybe this unknown lover was the man behind the murder of Pike, a murder for some reason that had nothing to do with the secret that Pike had shared with Standish. *Or maybe he didn't know that Pike had already told someone else.* Maybe he'd known that Pike had the information, but assumed that he was going to write about it rather than spilling it to the club chairman. Hale had suggested that to Dorothy and Tom that night at Murray's, but she'd steamed on with her own ideas.

"Was there any member that Flood seemed especially close to?"

"I'm not in the habit of noting the social habits of our waiters, Mr. Hale."

"No, of course not. But I bet that Mr. Blanton or one of the other waiters or somebody who works in the kitchen would know." That was what had brought him to Arthur's tonight to begin with. "I'd like to talk to them."

"I'm afraid I can't allow that. They're upset enough as it is, and it's hurting their work." Standish stood up. "I see that you've finished with your drink. I hope you enjoyed it. We must have drinks again sometime. But not soon, Mr. Hale."

Unwilling to burn any bridges behind him, Hale set down his empty glass on the bar without protest. "Thanks for the drink, and for the invitation. I'm sure we'll meet again."

Standish looked doubtful about that, despite his own suggestion.

Hale was passing through an empty corridor when he heard his name called in a low voice behind him. He turned around to see a waiter that he remembered from his previous visit to Arthur's—a rather bent old man with a white goatee. As he watched, the man stood taller. An amazing metamorphosis took place. Wrinkles smoothed out and the chin moved forward, the hairline appeared to rise, and the eyes widened as the face released its tension. Hale stopped himself just short of crying out in surprise.

"Meet me at Berkeley Square in twenty minutes," said Sherlock Holmes. "I have much to tell you."

EIGHTEEN
The Seven Solutions of Sherlock Holmes

Civilization is a conspiracy.
— John Buchan

Berkeley Square was about two long blocks north of Arthur's, very open with lots of park benches. It was bisected by two walking paths, one running north-south, the other east-west. Strollers liked to look at the statue of the nymph with the water jug or the house at number 50, said to be the most haunted house in London. And didn't Bertie Wooster live along here somewhere?

Hale settled himself into a chair at an outdoor table in front of Gunter's Tea Shop at number 7-8. The legendary shop, dating back to 1799, was famous for its ice creams with exotic flavors like maple, pineapple, white coffee, elderflower, Parmesan, and lavender. Hale ordered tea and pondered what the devil Holmes was up to.

Precisely at the end of the appointed twenty minutes, Sherlock Holmes sauntered casually by, still in character, wearing the goatee and the suit of the waiter who had been at Arthur's. Hale quickly set down his teacup and walked beside him.

"I suppose you think you're investigating," Holmes said.

"Well, somebody should," Hale snapped.

"I'm drawing my nets, Hale."

"Flood didn't kill himself, did he?"

"By no means. The writer of that so-called suicide note made a fair attempt at copying Flood's hand, but the agitation of a man about to kill himself doesn't account for the copperplate 's.' It's quite dissimilar to the one on the note that Flood wrote to his mother.

"We know from the genuine note that Flood was right-handed. That's supported by the whiskey stain on the floor which indicates that Flood was holding a drink in his right hand when he was shot."

"I think I remember him pouring tea with his right hand at Arthur's."

"Most likely he did. But the position of the pistol is more consistent with a left-handed shooter, and yet too far from the body. In order to shoot himself in the heart with his left hand, he would have to use his thumb. If he had done so the pistol would not have reloaded itself and reset the hammer. The pistol must be held in a rigid hand to cycle properly, which cannot be done if firing with the thumb in such an awkward position. The pistol has functioned properly, therefore it was held in a firm hand.

"The cartridge has a head-stamp marking that shows it was made by the Remington Arms Co. of Ilion, N.Y. Millions of such rounds were imported by our Government during the Great War, and thousands were stolen from U.S. ships docking in Ireland."

"Ireland! Then my idea about the IRA—"

"Was certainly very creative. Your explanation for the travel brochures fits in well with that theory, but I think it more likely that Flood was contemplating a honeymoon at some point in the distant future. I've learned that he had a young lady by the name of Bessie O'Casey, a pretty young Irish girl who works in the kitchen at Arthur's. We've become friends rather quickly, Bessie and I. Apparently I remind her of a favorite uncle. 'We were truly in love, sir,' she assured me. 'He wouldn't go anywhere without me.' She lowered her voice in a conspiratorial fashion. 'And he wouldn't be going anywhere *with* me either any time soon, what with me being in a family way.' Then she burst out weeping and said that they'd been to confession and they were going to get Mrs. Flood's favorite priest, a Father O'Connor, to break the happy news to her so she wouldn't have to hear it from her beloved son."

Hale almost objected that Flood's romantic interests lay in another direction, but he had known men who weren't particular in that regard.

"She also swore that Flood had nothing to do with those IRA devils, nor would he have killed himself. 'Never in a million years, sir.'"

"Then what was her explanation?"

"It wasn't easy to get Bessie to opine on that, but I finally got it out of her. 'I think somebody gave him a lot of pounds to do it,' she said. 'He thought we needed money, you see, so he could marry me and give our child a name. I kept telling him we didn't really need money. We had everything important, but I couldn't convince him of that. So it's my fault that he did that terrible thing, and my fault that he's dead.' She was being quite irrational, but try to tell a wailing woman that."

The poor girl! Hale felt doubly sympathetic knowing that she had confided all of this to Sherlock Holmes, of all people. "Then whoever paid Flood must have also killed him."

"You are scintillating this evening, Hale. Not even Watson could have stated the obvious more succinctly."

Hale wanted to punch the aging sleuth. How had Watson resisted the urge to do that all those years? Or had he? Maybe he didn't tell everything in those stories of his. "If it was so obvious, why didn't you say all of this on Saturday?"

"I would have much preferred that the murderer of Timothy Flood go on thinking that his staged suicide had us fooled. If you haven't ruined that plan by your continued interference, I shall be very much surprised. Your journalistic enterprise isn't going to make the hunt any easier, Hale."

"You mean you haven't figured it out yet?"

"I can think of seven separate solutions, but I am particularly intrigued by the fact that Pike drank no ordinary tea, but Black Sage Tea from the Caribbean."

"Wait a minute." Hale looked at Holmes square in the face. "Whenever you told Watson that kind of thing—'seven separate solutions'—he just swallowed it without question. I'm not so easy. What are all these possible solutions? And I want to hear seven, not six."

Holmes sighed. "Very well, Hale, just for your entertainment I will enumerate the possibilities. One: The killer of Langdale Pike—by which I mean the individual behind Flood—was a member or a staff member of Arthur's who was avenging some offense. That has the virtue of proximity to the murder scene. Two: The killer was an outsider to Arthur's with a similar motive. Three: The killer removed Pike to prevent him from seeing something that was going to happen across the street where Pike would see it from his place in the bow window—"

"Dorothy suggested that," Hale interrupted, "but even she said it didn't seem very promising. We never followed up on it. She's almost obsessed with the idea that her colleague Smythe-Dickey is involved."

They began walking again.

"I'd like to meet that Miss Sayers. Four: The killer was Pike's rival, either in love or in business, who could no longer endure the competition. Five: The killer acted to protect a secret that Pike had uncovered. Six: The killer was a family member or lover motivated by either passion or greed. And, finally, seven: The killer is you, Hale. You were, after all, with him when he died."

Before he could work up an outrage, Hale realized that the unemotional Holmes wouldn't eliminate Watson himself from a suspect list just because of friendship.

"And why would I kill Pike?" he asked.

"Because Pike gave you a valuable piece of information for a story and you wanted to make sure he didn't tell anyone else. Or perhaps your own star would shine the brighter if the source of your information was hidden forever in a tomb."

"That's a terrible motive! Edgar Wallace wouldn't dare use that in a novel."

Holmes shrugged. "Well, I don't insist on it. Perhaps you had a different motive—revenge or romantic jealousy."

"What were you saying about Pike's special tea? Anybody who ever had tea with him would know that's what he drank."

"Doubtless that is true, but—"

What happened to keep Holmes from finishing the sentence came so fast that Hale wasn't even sure later about the order of events. There was the sound of a window shattering in a house across the park, the rush of air as a bullet sped by him, Sherlock Holmes pulling him down, and a sound that Hale recognized as being indisputably that of a gunshot.

Holmes and Hale were both on the ground and in the open. Pure adrenaline and experience from the Great War drove Hale now. The only cover was the large trees to their left. Without effort he grabbed the old man and half lifted him from the ground, driving both of them forward to the concealment.

Kneeling behind the tree, Holmes's jacket shoulder still in his hand, Hale scanned for the shooter. He knew how hard it was to find a sniper, but one in a city was doubly hard. The echoes created by the canyons of buildings played hell with finding the direction from where the shot came.

"You have certainly stirred up the killer behind Flood, my friend." Holmes was brushing off his coat as he got up.

Hale, still looking around, also slowly rose, clinging close to the large oak as he did so.

"Me?"

"If you will remember, you were the one asking questions in all the obvious places."

"Look, Holmes, that was a high-powered rifle. I know the crack as the bullet passes close to your head. It travels at speeds beyond sound. Only those who've never been shot at talk about the whiz of bullets. The glass broke to our right, then came the sound of the shot, so it had to come from a distance—from over toward those buildings would be my guess." Hale pointed from behind the tree.

"There may be hope for you yet, Hale. You do have keen observation and some deductive powers. Now, if you don't mind, we shall continue our walk. It is quite safe, I assure you. The killer won't try again until later."

Something to look forward to, thought Hale.

NINETEEN
Rival

You know my methods. Apply them.
— Sherlock Holmes, *The Sign of Four*

"Sherlock Holmes saved my life by pulling me down," Hale reported the next morning.

Rathbone studied his bent pipe. "That's a bit of an embarrassment, isn't it? The old duffer must be about— what, seventy years old?"

"Sixty-eight, I think. But he's always been very athletic. And I did help him, too."

"Yes. Well. Apparently you've stirred up a hornet's nest."

"That's what Holmes said. I think it's safe to assume that somebody took umbrage at the questions I've been asking. Whoever it was shot from behind a building and got away clean. It's hard for me not to take that personally."

"Good, because I want a first-person account."

"It's right here." Hale handed over the typed pages. "I stayed up half the night writing it after I got back from Scotland Yard."

"You don't scare easily, do you? Good man." Rathbone settled in for a long read. The story began with a dramatic account of the shooting before reporting what Hale had learned at Arthur's and from Holmes earlier in the evening:

> It has been said that one of the most exhilarating experiences in life is to be shot at and missed. That's true—but only after it's over. During the experience, one is just scared.
>
> I know because it happened to me last night in the middle of Berkeley Square. I felt the bullet go past me before I heard the sound.

Near the end of the story, Rathbone looked up. "Did you get Holmes's permission to report his seven possible solutions?"

"He didn't tell me not to use it." *I didn't ask.* "You'll notice that I didn't blow his cover. It reads like he's being quoted as an expert on crime who knew the victim, not as someone who's actively involved in an investigation."

Rathbone went back to reading, asking no further questions until the end. He occasionally changed a word or two.

"Well done, Hale," he said at the end. "But don't get any ideas about asking for combat pay."

"No, sir." He recognized Rathbone's brisk comment for what it was, a manly way of acknowledging that Hale had almost taken a hit in service to the Central Press Syndicate.

"Where do you go from here?" Rathbone said. "It's all very well for the great detective to say that there are seven possible solutions, but that doesn't really help a lot, does it? Six of them are rather broad and the seventh is—you!"

Hale smiled. "I've ruled me out, sir. But when I was going over my notes for the story, one of the other six struck me as being worth follow-up. It was the idea that the killer is a rival of Pike's."

"Do you think his Miss Grayson had another admirer?"

Hale shuddered inwardly. "That's possible, I suppose, but I was thinking about a professional rival. Aloysius Bone showed up at Arthur's almost before Pike's body was cold. It's clear that he's trying to assume the dead man's mantle in the world of the trash papers. Maybe he's not just capitalizing on the situation but brought it about. And he knew about me getting coshed. Maybe I accepted his word too easily when he told me that he found out about the attack on me from Harker. I'll have to ask Harker, but I haven't seen him this morning."

"You won't. I chased him off." Hale's face must have registered surprise. "Well, he was becoming a bloody nuisance." Rathbone's tone was defensive.

"I understand, sir. Do you think he's gone for good?"

The managing director shook his head mournfully. "I don't think we'll be that lucky."

"I can track him down if it becomes necessary. But I don't need to do that before I talk to Bone. There's something else I want to ask him about, too—regarding Mr. Harrison Scott."

A few minutes later, a she pulled his mail out of the slot with his name on it, Hale formulated a preliminary plan. He didn't want to wait until the midnight hour to look for Bone at The 43, but he knew that the man also spent time at the Drones Club. Hale was trying to decide what time to show up there when a typed envelope with no return address caught his attention.

He opened it, slitting it with a silver letter opener that Sadie had given him for his birthday. Inside was a single sheet of paper. Hale's eyes went immediately to the bottom, where he registered the lack of a signature. The short message in the middle of the page read:

MR. "REGINALD SMYTHE-DICKEY" IS NOT WHO HE APPEARS TO BE. YOU SHOULD INVESTIGATE.

A FRIEND

Smythe-Dickey! Could Dorothy possibly have been on the right track with what Hale had thought was a ridiculous obsession with her co-worker? If he wasn't who he claimed to be, who was he? *Oh, God, please don't let him be another Secret Service agent!*

Hale had to go back to Benson's. There was no alternative. He would see Dorothy Sayers first. Although she had come into his life as an unbidden intrusion, the prospect of seeing her again was not at all unpleasant.

But first, Hale spent twenty minutes with the CPS librarian, Trosley. There was no record of a Reginald Smythe-Dickey anywhere, not even in the London telephone directory.

"Hello, Dorothy."

She looked up from a set of page proofs on her desk and regarded Hale with a sparkle in her bright blue eyes.

"Well, you don't look any the worse for wear," she said in her loud voice. "Been shot at yet today?"

"Not shot, but I did get a bit of a shock." He handed her the typed message. She barely glanced at it before giving it back to him.

"Well, I can't say I'm surprised."

"I think I'd better talk to Smythe-Dickey. Is he in?"

"Am I my brother's keeper? Let's go see."

The copywriter's office was empty.

"Watch the door while I look around," Hale said.

Without a word of protest, Dorothy stood in the doorway as Hale poked and prodded amid proof sheets, sketch pads, and sample products.

"Nothing incriminating," he reported after a ten-minute search.

"What do we do now?" she asked.

He looked at his watch. It was almost lunchtime. "I'm going to stop by a private club called the Drones, never mind why. Sorry, but you can't tag along this time. They wouldn't let you in. Will you be here this afternoon?"

"Of course. Slaving over a hot pen."

"I'll be back. We may yet have our conversation with Mr. Smythe-Dickey."

TWENTY
Drones

It is the public scandal that offends; to sin in secret is no sin at all.
— Molière

The Drones Club was located in Mayfair on Dover Street, off of Piccadilly, a location that firmly relegated it to the second string among clubs since it was neither on St. James's Street nor Pall Mall. Still, its neighbors included the Junior Naval and Military Club, the Bath Club, the Scottish Club, and the Arts Club—not such bad company.

As Hale looked around at the generally younger crowd of idle rich and semi-rich men, having used Bone's name to gain entrance, he knew why the aspiring gossipmonger spent some of his daylight hours here. Although the members traveled on the fringes of the best circles, making them a good source of information for Bone, many were often in need of a small loan to tide them over. The likes of Pongo Twistleton or Bingo Little would be shocked at the idea of providing gossip to the gossip papers, of course. But for the expenditure of a five- or ten-pound loan and the cost of a couple of drinks, Bone could suck the nitwits dry of juicy tidbits without them even noticing.

When Hale entered one of the two smoking rooms, he immediately saw Bone talking to Alexander Charles "Oofy" Prosser, a homely individual with a pimple-marked face who was the only true millionaire in the club. Hale marked time by looking idly out the window at the Messrs Thorpe & Briscoe Coal Company offices and the Demosthenes Club. Within a few minutes he saw that Bone was free and he casually wandered over to him.

"Hello, Aloysius," he said cheerfully.

The little man did not seem pleased to see him. "What are you doing here? Must you follow me everywhere?"

"Is that any way to talk to your guest?"

Bone gulped the cocktail in his hand—a sidecar, if Hale wasn't mistaken. "What do you want this time?"

"I want some answers, and they'd better be good ones. Certain people knew that I was asking about Harrison Scott." He looked around and lowered his voice. "Let's not be coy. I'm talking about the Holmes brothers. They like to act like they know everything, but they have to get their information somewhere. Since I'm pretty sure that Ned Malone didn't tell them I was curious about Scott, I figure it must have been you. Why did you spill the beans on me? I'm mighty tempted to think that you wanted to shut me down, and one good reason for that would be if you were behind Pike's murder."

Hale's attempt to sound subtly threatening was wasted on Bone. In fact, he seemed to relax a little. "You're crazy, Hale. Murder? Me? And I don't even know any Holmes brothers. Look, I know there's something not quite right about Scott. I don't know what it is—a connection with gangsters, or spies, or something. But I do know that he likes his privacy. I figured that if I tipped him off that somebody was asking about him he would appreciate it and that would pay off for me later. A guy like that must know something that I could use."

For all the secrecy of His Majesty's Secret Service, Hale and M were apparently on the same side in this case. Maybe the old spymaster would be willing to tell him whether what Bone just said was true. But it didn't really matter, did it?

"Whoever you told," Hale said, "you were trying to get me in trouble and off the story. Weren't you?"

Bone licked his lips. "Well, I have to admit that I wouldn't mind getting a piece of the story myself, and that's pretty hard with you in the way. A story like that, it could be my big break."

Break? Hale wanted to break his neck.

"What would you say if I told you that Harker denies telling you about me being coshed?"

"I'd say that old fool is a damned liar," Bone responded hotly. "Or maybe he just forgot. I think he's losing it."

Hale wasn't sure that Harker had ever had it. Studying Bone, he reached the reluctant conclusion that he was almost certainly telling the truth—at least about the attack on Hale and the theft of Pike's notebook. But what if the murderer had nothing to do with that? Maybe somebody else had secrets to protect and thought that Pike might have written them down. Hale was reluctant to give up the notion of the distasteful Bone as a murder suspect.

"You know, Aloysius, it has not escaped Scotland Yard's attention that Pike's death has been a boost to your career," he lied.

Bone snorted. "Don't I wish! I did think it would create an opening with some of Pike's regular outlets, like *The Daily Graphic*, *The Star*, or *The Daily Mirror*, but no such luck yet. I need something to grab their attention. You could help your old friend Aloysius, you know. Throw me a bone." He chuckled at his own wit. "I mean, you must have found out something that a respectable organization like the Central Press Syndicate wouldn't let you report."

You mean like the truth about Pike's socialist sister who isn't his sister?

"If I did, I wouldn't give it away for free," Hale said, "but I might be willing to trade it to you. Do you know anything about a fellow named Reginald Smythe-Dickey?"

Bone looked thoughtful, or as close as he could come, but at length he shook his curly head. "I don't think so. Who is he? Somebody in society?"

"He looks like he could be. It's been suggested to me that he may not be who he says he is. He works at Benson's, the big advertising outfit."

"I'll ask around. If I come up with anything, I'll let you know."

"You do that. There could be a little something in it for you. As I said, a trade."

Hale started to leave.

"Wait a minute. Aren't you staying for lunch in the dining room?"

The thought of eating with Bone upset his stomach. And Bone would expect him to pay the 6s 9d. "Not today, Aloysius. I have a date with a lady."

TWENTY-ONE
The Unmasking

We are so accustomed to disguise ourselves to others that
in the end we become disguised to ourselves.
– Francois de La Rochefoucauld

In truth, Hale didn't have a date, but he did have a
hope. Perhaps Dorothy would be free for lunch. He had to
circle back to Benson's anyway to see if Smythe-Dickey had
returned to his office.

She was so excited to see him that she almost
dropped her cigarette.

"He's here!" she said, even louder than her usual
wake-the-dead voice.

"You mean Reggie?"

"Of course I mean Reggie! We must beard the lion
in his den." *So much for lunch. Maybe later.* "What's your
plan?"

Plan? "It's . . . evolving. Something tells me that
you're a good actress, so go along with whatever I say. Just
trust me."

Dorothy stood up. "You're not the first man who's
said that to me. I hope this works out better than it usually
does."

So did Hale.

They found Reginald Smythe-Dickey in his office, pen in hand, concentrating on a newspaper. The forehead above his pince-nez was wrinkled in thought.

"Oh, there you are, Reggie!" Dorothy announced, as though she'd been looking high and low throughout what was left of the British Empire. "Hard at work, I see."

His head jerked up, a startled look on his face, but he recovered quickly. "I certainly am. What's a six-letter word for 'detective'?"

Hale said "Holmes" and Dorothy said "sleuth" almost in unison.

All of a sudden, Hale had the idea that he'd been groping for, the way to find out whether Smythe-Dickey was the imposter that Dorothy theorized. He shut the door and spoke quickly, urgently. "This is no time for crossword puzzles, Reggie. They're on to you. You'll never get out of this mess alive without a friend or two to help, and Miss Sayers and I are just the ones to do it."

Smythe-Dickey's green eyes widened. Where had Hale seen eyes like those before? "Who's on to me? What mess? What the devil are you babbling about, Hale?"

Dorothy stood behind him mouthing, "Yes, what?"

Now Hale had a choice of wild accusations to throw, hoping to panic the man into admitting something. What should it be—drugs or theft? Hale settled on the more exotic route.

"The cops know that you're the Black Mask, the gentleman-thief responsible for half a dozen daring burglaries in Hyde Park this year alone." Hale tried to sound like what he imagined an American gangster would sound like. He'd stolen the Black Mask name from an American crime magazine that Tom Eliot liked to read. Behind Smythe-Dickey, Dorothy rolled her eyes. "We can help you get the jewels to Marseilles," Hale went on.

"What'll it be, us or Scotland Yard? You'd better make up your mind fast, because Chief Inspector Wiggins is on his way here now."

"That's, that's . . . rubbish! It's insane. I'm no Black Mask. I'm Reginald Smythe-Dickey, copywriter for S.H. Benson."

"Who are you trying to convince, pal? That may be your name now, but Reginald Smythe-Dickey didn't exist until Benson's hired you." That was just a guess; in for a penny, in for a pound. But it was certainly true that his name didn't appear in the files of any London newspaper.

Dorothy put a hand on her copywriting colleague's shoulder. "Reggie, or whoever you really are, don't you see? It's no use pretending with us." Her voice was soft and sultry, two qualities Hale had never previously associated with Dorothy L. Sayers. How could any man resist?

Smythe-Dickey didn't resist.

"I tell you I don't know what you're talking about! I'm no thief." He stood and attempted to look taller than his five-ten, sticking out his thin, aristocratic nose. "My name is Charles Bridgewater, and I am the son of the Earl of Sedgewick."

It took a moment for it to register on Hale that this man was claiming to be the disinherited brother of his beloved Sadie—or rather, of her alter ego, Lady Sarah Bridgewater. When the words sank it, Hale felt strangely detached, as if he were in a theater watching a melodrama.

"That can't be," he mumbled.

"Why not?" Dorothy demanded.

"I happen to know that the Earl's son is missing."

"I'm not missing—I'm right here!" He took off his pince-nez, which made him look slightly less foolish. "Look, this is all a bit embarrassing. The truth is that I've had a bit of a falling out with the Governor. I came back from the War in a bad way, nerves shot and all that. I got into some bad habits—drinking, gambling, even drugs. I ran with a wild crowd."

"And your father didn't approve," Dorothy said.

Bridgewater's chuckle had a bitter edge. "You could say that. He gave me the old heave-ho—fired me from my position on the estate and cut off my allowance. Didn't leave me much alternative, did he? I had to find a way to earn a few pounds on my own. Well, how hard could that be? Other johnnies less talented than me do it. I'd always been rather good with words, so I thought I'd take a whack at the advertising game. But I couldn't use my own name. That would infuriate the Governor to a point where I'd never get back into his good graces."

It was no coincidence that Benson's name had appeared in Pike's notebook, Hale realized. He had asked Pike to see if he could find out what happened to Lady Sarah's wastrel brother. Apparently he had succeeded, or at least had a line on it that he had written down with the intention of pursuing. And that could mean . . .

"You killed Pike to conceal your identity," Hale accused.

"Pike?" He stared blankly. "Who's that?"

"Oh, come on, Bridgewater, it's overplaying your hand to pretend that you don't even know about the murder," Hale snapped. "The papers have been full of it for a week."

"I only read the crossword puzzles."

"A man who traded in secrets was poisoned at his club just a week ago today," Dorothy said. "You, my dear colleague, are a man with a secret that you might well kill to protect."

"Nonsense. It's not even that big a secret. Philip Benson knows who I am. We used to play whist together. That's how I got the job. Even my sister knows, although I made her promise not to tell the Governor."

"Sarah? I don't believe it." She had told Hale that her father and brother were estranged. Why wouldn't she have mentioned that she and Charles were still on good terms? But then again, by unspoken consent, they didn't talk much about her family.

Bridgewater stared at Hale with those eyes that were so much like his sibling's. "How did you know my sister's name is Sarah?"

Hale was in no mood to explain. "I am a journalist and it's my job to know what other people don't know." Where had he read something like that? It didn't actually make a lot of sense. A journalist's real job is to find out things that the public should know, and then make sure that they know it.

"You didn't sound like a journalist a few minutes ago," Bridgewater said. "You sounded like some sort of criminal. I think Scotland Yard would be very interested to know about you."

"Give them a call," Hale said on his way out the door.

That couldn't make matters any worse.

TWENTY-TWO
Baker Street

Knowledge is not knowledge until someone else knows
that one knows.
— Lucilious, *Fragment*

"I don't hate the man, even though he is a liar,"
Dorothy insisted over lunch at the Museum Tavern across
from the British Museum. "I actually find his incompetence
rather endearing. But he could still be behind Pike's murder.
Nothing he said, even if it's all true, ruled that out."

"What about Lydia Grayson?" Hale said. "You
haven't eliminated her as a suspect, have you?"

"Didn't I mention that? As it happens, we have a
mutual friend. She assured me that Miss Grayson and Pike
were a strange couple but totally devoted to each other, and
to this mad cause of theirs."

Hale shook his head. "You continue to amaze me.
All right, then, let's get back to Bridgewater. There's an
aspect of this that I haven't had time to think about until
now: Whoever sent that anonymous letter wanted us to

investigate your colleague. Maybe it was the killer, trying to throw us off the scent."

Dorothy waved away the notion as though it were an annoying fly. "More likely it was a public-spirited person trying to do you a good turn. We need to find out whether anyone matching Bridgewater's description was talking to Flood within a few days of the murder, either at Arthur's or at his home."

"You want me to go back to Arthur's and ask questions again? No thanks. I'm not welcome there. And remember, I've been coshed and shot at already on this case. Even a cat has only nine lives."

As the image of Mrs. Flood's crying face popped into his head, Hale found the prospect of talking to her equally unappealing.

"Don't be silly." The way Dorothy said it immediately made Hale feel silly. "Why *should* you go there? Sherlock Holmes didn't say he was abandoning his disguise as a waiter at the club, did he?"

"No, but—"

"Good. He can ask the questions. We just have to get him to do it. Did he tell you where he's staying while he's in London?"

Hale smiled. "Take a guess."

"The Langham Hotel?"

"Number 221B Baker Street."

"His old flat?"

"He told me he continued to rent the place for many years after he left London. He used it as a secret refuge. More recently he bought the house from Mrs. Hudson. He said he was afraid someone else might purchase it and turn it into a museum."

"What a quaint notion. Well, it's not far. I'll give you a ride on my motorcycle."

"Couldn't we just walk?"

Less than ten harrowing minutes later, Hale found himself sitting in the famous sitting room at 221B Baker Street, waiting for Sherlock Holmes to get dressed for visitors.

"I thought it would be bigger," Dorothy said.

"Really? I thought it would be smaller." But the starting place for so many of Dr. Watson's adventures looked much as Hale had imagined it from those reports and the illustrations by Frederic Dorr Steel in *Collier's*. There was the wall defaced with bullet holes, although it took some imagination to read there the patriotic "V.R." that Watson had written of. But where was the Persian slipper full of tobacco? Where was the coal scuttle full of cigars?

"I took a few souvenirs of Baker Street with me to my home on the Downs many years ago," Holmes said briskly, striding into the room. "Oh, please, Hale, don't look so impressed. You make me feel like a mind reader on stage at the Alhambra. The direction of your eyes and the puzzlement on your face when you didn't see what you expected to see were as easy to read as this morning's *Times*. And this must be Miss Sayers. I've wanted to meet you."

"The desire is mutual, Mr. Holmes."

"I presume this visit is important, Hale. Not many people know that on rare occasions I still use this flat as a convenience. I should like to keep it like that." He glanced at Dorothy with his piercing gray eyes.

"Don't worry about me," she said. "I won't tell anybody. *He's* the reporter."

Ignoring her, Hale came to the point of their visit.

"Do you remember at the Diogenes Club when I told you everything I knew, and I said that Miss Sayers suspected her colleague, Reginald Smythe-Dickey, of being a phony?"

Holmes lit a pipe with a long, slightly bent stem. "Vividly. I'm retired, not senile."

"You should try to find out whether anybody at Arthur's saw him with Timothy Flood," Dorothy said.

"I've already made inquiries along that line, my dear lady. That gentleman is not a member of the club under any name, and no one at Arthur's recalled seeing a man of his description talking with Flood. Neither did Mrs. Flood."

Hale was speechless. He doubted if Dorothy ever was.

"Why did you do that?" she asked.

"Because it was an inquiry worth pursuing and Hale failed to pursue it. His energies were misdirected elsewhere."

"But how did you know what he looked like?" Hale said. "I didn't tell you."

"Oh, I simply asked Philip Benson, for whose father I once solved the theft of an egg."

"Faberge?" Dorothy asked.

"No, it was a common duck egg, utterly without value and yet totally priceless. That is what made the case so interesting."

G.K. Chesterton, the master of paradox, probably would have been delighted by such talk, but not Hale. He had no time for it. If Holmes had talked to Benson about "Smythe-Dickey" . . .

"Then you know who the fellow really is?" he demanded.

Holmes nodded. "Benson saw no reason not to tell me. But he told me in confidence."

"You could have at least let me know that he wasn't a suspect," Hale grumbled.

"May I remind you, Hale, that our last conversation was cut rather short by bullets aimed in your direction?"

Hale couldn't deny that, so he ignored it. "I wonder who sent me the anonymous letter?"

"Just some busybody," Dorothy said. "It's not important."

"Perhaps it is," Holmes said. "Do you still have the letter, Hale?"

"Right here." He pulled it out of his breast pocket and handed it to the detective.

After a moment's study, Holmes said, "It should be easy enough to find out who wrote it by identifying the typewriter used. It's not commonly known yet, but typewriting is as individualized as handwriting. The keys of each machine have their peculiarities. I've even written a small monograph on the subject."

"But how would you even know where to begin— what typewriters to match it against?" Hale asked.

"Elementary. We'll simply compare this letter to the typewriting of every employee of S.H. Benson's."

"Oh, stop it," Dorothy snapped. "You're toying with me, Holmes. You know I wrote the letter."

"Well, the thought had crossed my mind. This twenty-pound paper is similar to the letterhead stationary used at Benson's, and just enough paper has been cut off the top to eliminate that letterhead. Combining that knowledge with the fact that Hale said you were obsessed with Smythe-Dickey, there seemed little reason to look any further for our friend's anonymous correspondent."

Hale felt himself grow hot. Dorothy had made a fool of him. "Do you know what you need, Dorothy L. Sayers?"

"A good Scotch?"

"A good spanking, rather."

"Fortunately," said Holmes, "while other lines of investigation have turned into dead ends, my old associate Shinwell Johnson has not been idle. He was finally able to learn who coshed you, Hale. That particular nastiness was the handiwork of one Digger Dalton, a veteran bruiser of no great subtlety. Whenever one of the gangs of London needs somebody for a rough job, possibly with a spot of robbery for seasoning, Digger is high on their call list."

Hale could hardly contain his excitement. "That's the game, then. All we have to do is find him, or get Scotland Yard to find him, and make him talk."

"It's not quite that simple, I'm afraid. First of all, not talking is Digger's secondary specialty after inflicting physical harm. And secondly, he's disappeared. Word among his more loquacious comrades is that he may have left the country for a while."

So close, and yet so far, Hale thought.

"Then we haven't gotten anywhere," Dorothy said.

"The situation is not so grim as all that, Miss Sayers. Quite the contrary. Don't you see the implications of Digger's involvement?"

Hale and Dorothy looked at each other blankly.

"No? Well, perhaps I have the advantage of experience that allows me to add that information to one or two other indications and come up with the solution. There's a bigger crime than murder here, or perhaps I should say a more far-reaching one."

"You mean you think you know what this is all about and who's behind it?" Hale asked. *Or are you just posturing to impress us?*

"I'm quite sure of it." Holmes pulled out a pocket watch. "In several hours I shall know for sure, if the whispers that Porky Shinwell picked up are correct."

"What are you talking about?" Hale found Holmes's penchant for acting mysteriously much more entertaining when he was reading about it in a magazine story.

"I should rather not say. Even though the good Watson is otherwise occupied tonight, I can still hear him whispering 'Norbury' in my ear to keep me from being overconfident of my powers. But if you'd care to join me and friend Wiggins later, you may witness a criminal conspirator caught in the act."

"Join you where?"

"On the Royal Victoria Dock."

TWENTY-THREE
From Dancing to the Docks

It is the character of a brave and resolute man not to be
ruffled by adversity and not to desert his post.
        – Cicero, *De Officiis*

"It's getting late," Hale said as he and Dorothy
emerged into the darkness. "Can I see you home?"

"I'm not going home. But you can take me to The
43. I've never been there, but it sounds like fun from your
description. I think that would be a jolly place to wait until
we meet up with Holmes, don't you? We'll be just like the
Three Musketeers, you and me and Holmes. I'll be Athos."

Damn the woman, anyway!

Hale took a deep breath to calm down. "I'm sorry,
Dorothy, really I am, but you can't go along with me this
time."

"And why not?" She actually sounded surprised.

"It's too dangerous."

Dorothy stopped walking. "I see. Because I'm a
woman, you mean?"

"Well, yes, of course. Look, somebody has killed
two people already and almost shot me. I don't think he

would hesitate to add you to the list just because you're a member of the fair sex. I can't risk your neck."

Oh, damn. He shouldn't have mentioned her neck. It was far from her best feature, strongly resembling that of a swan.

"But that hardly makes sense, Enoch," Dorothy said. "I want to see this thing through. Whatever risk my lovely neck is subjected to, I'll be taking it, not you."

"But I'd feel responsible."

"I'm getting tired of this conversation." She looked down the largely deserted street. "I see there's a bobby on the corner. What do you think would happen if I threw myself into your arms and pretended to struggle while I yelled 'rape' at the top of my lungs?"

"You wouldn't dare!"

Dorothy opened her mouth and sucked in a lungful of air. Hale put a hand over her mouth. "All right, you unprincipled wench, have it your way. But don't blame me if I have to write your obituary tomorrow."

Tentatively, he took the hand away.

"I knew you'd see reason," Dorothy said. "By the way, I like to lead when I dance."

"Big surprise," Hale muttered.

She was such a good dancer—almost as good as Sadie and about an inch taller—that he didn't mind that she led.

"This place is deliciously decadent," she said. "Is everybody here frightfully rich and clever?"

"Some are just rich. Aloysius Bone is neither." Bone had approached them almost as soon as Mrs. Meyrick let them through. Hale managed to put the gossipmonger off quickly, while deliberately giving him the impression that Dorothy was paid company. She was much amused.

As the band swung into "Everybody's Doin' It," Hale maneuvered Dorothy's body so that she was facing a certain couple. "Do you see the good-looking guy dancing with the blonde and ogling the brunette?" he whispered in her ear. "He's not one of the Italian waiters."

"Oh, isn't that Valentino, the actor? Well, he's pretty enough, but not quite as handsome as you."

Hale felt an unexpected tingle at the compliment. Dorothy L. Sayers was a plain-looking woman with sparse hair and a loud voice. And yet, if he wasn't very careful . . .

"I think it's only fair to tell you that I'm engaged," he said.

"Not officially. And besides, Lady Sarah is on her way to Egypt. Out of sight, out of mind. But it was very noble of you to warn me."

He pulled away slightly. "How do you know about her?"

"Horace Harker told me. I asked him to tell me all about you the day we met."

"You little minx. You know Harker?"

"Not well, but he interviewed me when my first book of poetry was published. I'm surprised you didn't look me up in the CPS files."

"I'm not that sneaky," he huffed, "but I did buy your opus. I can honestly say it was the best book of poetry I ever bought."

"And the only one, I dare say."

They both laughed. Her laugh was louder.

"I did read it, though," he added. "I liked the last poem best. How did it go? 'The thing that I remember most of all. Is the white hemlock by the garden wall.'"

"I'm still rather fond of that one myself."

"And do you still miss Oxford?"

"I've never really left it."

"What would your Oxford mates say about you being up to your neck"—her neck again!—"in a murder mystery?"

"The old girls would be envious as hell. What do you think Holmes is up to?"

"You know as much as I do," Hale said. "But given the location of our rendezvous tonight, it doesn't sound like the killer is somebody from Arthur's."

Sherlock Holmes arrived first and sat in the dark, remembering earlier days and similar circumstances— waiting in the cellar of the City and Suburban Bank for John Clay, waiting in the bedroom at Stoke Moran for the attack of the Speckled Band, waiting at the house of the spy Hugo Oberstein for the wrong person in the Bruce-Partington affair. Watson had been with him then, every time. Watson had never let him down, not once. Good old, Watson, the one fixed point . . .

Until now. For the first time, Watson had begged off. Well, the man deserved whatever peace his domestic arrangements afforded him. He was seventy years old and long since retired with his latest wife. She could hardly be expected to understand how much Holmes needed Watson, really needed him. Perhaps Watson didn't understand either.

Well, Holmes wouldn't be alone. Wiggins would be here soon. How right Holmes had been with the faith he had placed in the younger Wiggins so long ago. He always knew that the street Arab could make something of himself. Maybe he would go all the way to the top, eventually succeeding Stanley Hopkins as Commissioner of the Yard.

But, friendship and old times aside, Wiggins was the official police and therefore no stand-in for Watson. No, that was Hale's role tonight. Hale had been furious with him at the end of the Hangman business. Holmes would have been disappointed in him if he hadn't been. The man had intelligence, determination, and courage. And he was an American. Holmes had always liked Americans.

The only thing Hale lacked was a gun. Holmes opened his revolver and checked his cartridges one more time.

He took a seat on a crate marked "gasoline engine" and checked his watch. It was nigh on two in the morning. Wiggins and Hale should be along shortly.

Below his position of vantage, the Royal Victoria Dock was a buzz of activity. It reminded Holmes of his bee hives. Winches and cranes were moving boxes labeled "jam" onto a coastal freighter. Victoria was now used largely for grain and meat shipping. Huge refrigerated warehouses and grain silos stood along the quays. The London Docks were used for other cargo, including the shipping of wine and liquor. They even had a huge cavern for the storage of wine casks out of the weather and in the cool darkness. With the onset of Prohibition in the States, the London Docks were well monitored. That's why the rum runners were using Victoria. Hale had been poking around the wrong docks in researching his stories on the illegal alcohol trade.

Holmes had told Wiggins and Hale to meet him on the east side of the Premier Mills Silo. From there they had a clear view of the freighter *Barn Swallow*.

Hearing the bang of a motorcycle engine in the distance, Holmes checked his watch again. That would be Hale. But to his astonishment, as the vehicle came into view he saw that a woman was driving.

"Good evening, Miss Sayers." Holmes managed a smile as the duo approached. "I see that Hale has not been able to dissuade you from coming on our little foray tonight."

"I had no intention of being left out of the fun, Mr. Holmes," she replied.

"Yes, well . . . here's Wiggins. Is all in place, Chief Inspector?"

Wiggins and a uniformed sergeant had joined the trio in the lee of the silo.

"Yes, sir. Reminds me of the old days and going after Mr. Small." Wiggins grinned, clearly waxing nostalgic. "I've got a police launch up river and another one down and a third at the entrance to the docks. They'll move in if Sergeant Bartel here fires a red flare. Just in case, you know."

"Excellent," replied Holmes. "Though I doubt our quarry will try a water escape."

"I've got a squad at the entrance to this quay and they'll close it off when I sound the whistle."

"Good. Then for now, we wait." Holmes settled back on his crate, his back against the silo wall.

"Excuse me, Mr. Holmes, but just what are we waiting for?" asked Dorothy.

"Do you see the gangplank from the freighter to the quay?"

"Certainly."

"Shortly, according to what Porky Shinwell was told by an old friend and former business collaborator of his, there will be a meeting there and money will change hands. That is what we are waiting for. Now, silence, I believe, is in order."

Dorothy was about to say something else, but Hale put his hand on her arm and led her a short distance away.

"Not much for talking, is he?" Dorothy whispered to Hale.

"Oh, he will be when it's all over. Then he loves to explain it all to those lesser mortals who haven't been able to figure out what he's doing."

"That's us, I guess."

"Psst . . ." Wiggins motioned for quiet and waved them back towards the packing crates. The pair hustled back. Crouching down with the others, they saw three men walking toward the gangplank. The men stopped under the lamplight. Another man, who appeared to be a ship's officer, approached the trio from the ship.

Hale watched the three men shake hands with the officer. Then one of the men stepped back a few paces and started scanning the quay while the others talked. One of the men was holding what appeared to be a tin box.

"Very professional, I must say," whispered Holmes. "They even brought their own lookout. You may assume the American is armed, Wiggins."

"I always assume Americans are armed, Mr. Holmes. There you are, they've passed the tin box. Time to move, sir."

"Hale, keep Miss Sayers here with you," Holmes said. "We will attempt to make an arrest without incident. Come Wiggins, you are the official police, after all."

Wiggins, Holmes, and the sergeant stood up and walked slowly toward the gangplank.

"Who the devil are those men?" asked Dorothy.

"I'm pretty sure I have a general idea, but I don't like the looks of this. You stay here. I'm going to circle around the silo and come up on the other side."

"Like hell I'll stay here! If you're going, so am I!"

Hale looked toward Holmes, Wiggins, and Sergeant Bartel. They were almost out into the light now; he couldn't afford to waste time arguing. Then it struck him: Standish! One of the men was George Standish! Somehow it all went back to Arthur's after all. "It's your funeral," he muttered to Dorothy. He took off at a trot around the silo, with Dorothy close behind. It was then that he heard the yell:

"Boss, it's a setup—coppers!" That must have been the lookout calling.

Another voice called out, "Dwyer, come back. Put down that gun, man. We can handle this." It was Standish, no doubt about it.

Hale was just coming around the other side of the silo when he heard the shot and the police whistle almost at the same time. As he broke onto the quay he could see the ship's officer and one man still standing at the gangplank. The other two were fleeing for the entrance to the dock, where a Ford automobile sat, engine running. The man who had been the lookout was hanging back, looking over his shoulder to make sure his employer was going to make it to the car. His gun was still pointed toward Holmes and Wiggins. The sergeant was on his knees—the first shot had found a mark. *There isn't going to be a second shot!* The thought flew through Hale's brain like lightning. He hurled himself on the man with the gun. The crook went down with a thud and the gun flew from his hand as his head hit the railroad track in the quay. Hale heard the gears of the Ford grind as its motor roared.

Hale was now swarmed by constables who cuffed the unconscious man on the ground as Holmes and Wiggins rushed up.

"I think my coach at Yale would have been proud of that open field tackle," Hale said as he slowly got off the ground, dusting himself off. Dorothy was just catching up.

"My motor!" she screamed. "They've run over my motor. Oh, they'll pay for this!" She shook a fist at the fleeing auto.

At least you were slow enough they didn't run you *over,* thought Hale.

"Damn, damn, damn," spat Wiggins. "He's driven right through my men. But we'll get him! Collins! Get the sergeant to hospital. Doesn't look too bad. Sorry, Mr. Holmes, my men will take care of Standish and the ship's captain. I've got to try and get Big Bill."

He ran off.

"Standish? Big Bill? What's going on, Mr. Holmes?" Dorothy demanded.

"We've solved the murders of Mr. Pike and Mr. Flood, broken up a gang of rum runners, and found that if Hale ever gives up journalism he could be a great rugby player. Watson played rugby for Blackheath, you know."

TWENTY-FOUR
Unraveling a Tangled Skein

No problem can stand the assault of sustained thinking.
– Voltaire

"It was perfectly obvious almost from the first that Timothy Flood was the killer," said Sherlock Holmes, "and equally obvious that there must be some Iago, some driving force behind him. It took me longer than it should have to find out whom and why."

"And the why went right back to my stories about rum runners in England and the United States," Hale said, thumping his hand on the table. "I should have been the first to see that, but I never made the connection between my illegal booze series and the murders of Langdale Pike and Timothy Flood."

Half of London —the half that read the newspapers— now knew that Pike had wanted to meet with Hale on the day he was murdered because he had somehow caught wind of Standish's involvement in the rum running trade. Having read Hale's stories on the subject, he knew that the American would want to hear what he'd learned. But George Standish, O.B.E., M.P., had had a different idea.

Later on the morning that Standish and the ship's captain had been arrested at the Royal Victoria Dock, Holmes fled London for his bees. Big Bill Dwyer had escaped. Being a man of foresight, he had had a plane waiting for just such an eventuality. After all, boats could be chased. Back in the capital almost two weeks later on some undisclosed business—perhaps for M, Hale speculated—Holmes had invited Hale, Dorothy, and Wiggins to dinner at Simpson's. Hale, who hadn't dined at the venerable restaurant since his farewell dinner with Sadie, accepted with the pleasurable anticipation of talking over the case.

Dorothy had replaced her motorcycle with a new one, but allowed Hale to pick her up in a cab. She wore a smashing scarlet dress and long earrings to match, with a multi-colored necklace of bright beads adorning her swan's neck.

The first part of the evening was purely social, peppered by talk of sport and politics. With the famous Simpson's beef enjoyed by all hands, the program had progressed to after-dinner drinks and discussion of the events that had brought the four of them together. Mostly they revisited old territory, in the way that friends and fellow-survivors are prone to do.

"Apparently Mr. Standish is a better politician than he is a businessman," Wiggins said, setting down his port. "His legitimate enterprises were sinking, so to speak, but Big Bill offered him a chance to make a lot of money with his ships, and none of it going to the Inland Revenue."

"Pike must have had some kind of confrontation with Standish or, more likely, asked him a few questions that made him suspicious." Hale lit a panatela. "That's why his name was in Pike's diary. When I asked Standish about that in our first meeting, he made up the story that Pike had met with him to report socially unacceptable behavior by a member. He built on that later, claiming that Flood was the other party in order to give Flood a motive for killing Pike."

"Nothing that we were able to learn about Flood from any other source gave the story credibility, however," Holmes pointed out. "Of course, Standish expected everyone to believe his story without question. Flood was just a young Irish waiter."

"Poor Flood!" Dorothy said from behind a wreath of cigarette smoke.

"Standish confessed that he paid Flood to put the prussic acid in the tea, telling him it was a joke—just something to make Pike a little sick," Wiggins said. "Flood was either a bit thick to believe that, or he wanted to believe it. After the murder, Standish blackmailed Flood into silence by telling him that nobody would believe his story and he would hang for the murder. But Flood was showing signs of a guilty conscience. Standish knew that he would crack eventually, no matter the consequences, so he had to go. Just like he thought you had to go, Mr. Hale, when you kept coming back to Arthur's to ask questions."

"Not that I got very close to the solution," Hale said ruefully. "How did you know that it was Standish, Holmes?"

"I wouldn't go so far as to call it elementary, but there were one or two indications in his direction early on. Standish made a mistake when he had Pike's diary stolen, probably assuming it contained an explicit account of what Pike had learned about him. It was no great leap for me to conclude that the killer's name was in that little book."

"But that didn't narrow it down much," Hale protested. "And we didn't know what was in the book except for the little bit that I remembered."

"When Standish took a shot at you—this time doing his own dirty work, I fancy—that was a clear indication to me that you were on to something with your inquiries," Holmes said. "So that's where I turned my attention—the ground that you'd already been over."

"Well, I'm sure that at least G.K.C. was never a suspect," Dorothy announced, "even though Enoch talked to him because his name was in the notebook."

Holmes shook his head. "On the contrary, my dear lady, Mr. Chesterton had excellent potential as a suspect. Because of his high profile as a thinker and writer on things theological, made all the more prominent by his recent reception into the Roman Church, any hint of scandal would be devastating to his reputation. That would be a strong motivation for murder."

Dorothy looked aghast.

"However," Holmes went on, "my associate Mercer was able to confirm that Chesterton hadn't been to London since his lunch with Pike, which meant that he had no opportunity to hire Flood. Nor had Flood's mother ever seen him in her son's company."

"Now wait a minute," Hale said. "Not that I ever suspected Chesterton, but how could you be sure he didn't go to London unnoticed and meet Flood somewhere away from Arthur's or the Flood home?"

"G.K. Chesterton never goes unnoticed," Dorothy said. "There's hardly a more recognizable man in the country."

"Benson's was also mentioned in the notebook and followed up by you, Hale," Holmes went on. "I've already told you how I ruled out the pseudonymous Mr. Smythe-Dickey."

"But how did you know it wasn't somebody else at Benson's—like Miss Sayers here," Wiggins said with an unaccustomed twinkle in his eye.

"When Porky Shinwell found out that Digger Dalton stole Pike's diary or notebook, call it what you will, that immediately suggested the involvement of organized crime. Lady copy-writers do not hire thugs . . . as a rule."

"Neither do members of Parliament!" Hale burst out.

"One might if he owns a failing shipping company that's involved in smuggling alcohol to America," Holmes replied calmly. "Mercer's inquiries established to my satisfaction that G. Standish Shipping Ltd. should have been bankrupt based on the amount of business it was doing.

"You will recall, Hale, that I was intrigued by Pike's affinity for Caribbean Black Sage Tea. You quite correctly observed that anyone who had tea with Pike would know about that particular preference. But not everyone would know what the tea would taste like—that it was strong enough to cover the bitter-almond flavor of prussic acid. But a man whose ships plied the Caribbean might."

"Cuba, to be specific," Hale said. "His ships went to Cuba. I knew that. Churchill even mentioned that Standish shared his love of Cuban cigars. It's no big stretch to think that he liked Caribbean tea as well, although I never saw Standish at teatime. Pike mentioned to me shortly before he died that somebody recommended the Black Sage Tea for his gout. That had to have been Standish."

"Not with homicidal intentions, I'm sure," Holmes said. "It must have been only later that he realized the tea would make a perfect delivery system for prussic acid."

"Pike was killed to hide a secret," Dorothy said. "That was one of your seven possible solutions that Enoch wrote about. So bravo! You were right. But what about your other six solutions? It doesn't seem to me that you gave them all equal consideration. What about the possibility that Pike was removed so that he wouldn't see something happen across the street, for example?"

"Or what about the possibility that friend Hale killed Pike so that he could be the exclusive holder of some valuable information that Pike had shared with him?" Holmes countered with a smile. "I never intended to imply that all seven theories were equally worthy of consideration, Miss Sayers. Several were ruled out either by the theft of the notebook or the identity of the thief, a professional criminal highly unlikely to have been hired by, oh, Sir James Forrester, for example."

"Forrester!" Hale smacked himself in the head. "Well, I never claimed to be a detective—and a damned good thing."

Three pairs of eyes regarded him quizzically.

"Forrester strongly implied to me that Standish wasn't on the up and up," Hale explained. "But I didn't take him seriously. I thought that was just sour grapes."

TWENTY-FIVE
Lady Sarah Demurs

A wise man is never surprised.
– Samuel Johnson, *The Rambler*

Over the next several weeks, Hale got swept up in Dorothy's project to help Timothy Flood's pregnant girlfriend. The plan involved sending Bessie O'Casey off to Ivy Shrimpton, Dorothy's cousin in Oxford, who agreed to let her come to term there.

"Ivy is just who I'd turn to if I were preggers," Dorothy announced with typical certitude.

And then, to Hale's puzzlement and disappointment, but also a measure of relief, Dorothy gradually faded from his life. He only saw her every couple of weeks for a friendly lunch. It was as if Enoch were a chapter of her life that she had closed, but occasionally paged through now and again. Perhaps she was busy with plans for a new career now that her mystery novel had been sold. (It would appear between covers as *Whose Body?* rather than *The Singular Adventure of the Man with the Golden Pince-Nez.*) Or maybe she had a lover.

Whatever the reason, he didn't see Dorothy very often as the summer wore on. Without the distraction of her panache, one of the most vibrant personalities he had ever known, Hale's feelings about Sadie became even stronger. He made up his mind that he would propose marriage to Lady Sarah Bridgewater as soon as he saw her again—and to hell with her father, her brother, Alfie Barrington, and the entire fussy old House of Lords!

As the weeks went by, it seemed that time would never arrive. But eventually, August gave way to September. It was toward the end of that month that Lady Sarah and her father steamed home on the *La Paloma.*

Hale was at the docks when they arrived, waiting anxiously for the first sight of his love coming off the ship. Was it only his imagination or had the proclamations of affection in her letters become rather perfunctory over the last couple of months? Maybe her father was reading them and she felt the need to be discreet. Or maybe some gossip had written to her about Dorothy and completely misrepresented their relationship. Her brother, who had reconciled with Sedgewood long-distance after his failure to thrive at Benson's, was the most obvious suspect. If Charles did that . . .! Or maybe some busybody got wind of the financial support he had provided to Bessie and her baby and started a rumor. Well, he could explain that, and Dorothy would back him up.

All these thoughts collided in his head for the hundredth time as he twisted his hat nervously, watching the first-class passengers descend from the ship. What a proper lot of toffs, as the British would say. He scanned the faces, looking for Sadie. *There she was!* She wore a wide-brimmed hat, turned up in the front, and a kit-fox colored wrap of Tarquina (kind of a velvet material) with Mandarin sleeves. The cuffs and upstanding collar were of real kit-fox. She looked every inch the returning Lady Sarah. Hale waved like an idiot, jumping up and down to catch her attention.

She saw him, smiled, and waved back. Hale felt a warm glow inside. Why had he ever thought there was anything to worry about?

A few minutes later, he was hugging her as if he would never let go.

"Darling, I just have one question to ask you," he began. This was it. He wouldn't wait a moment longer to propose.

But Sadie pulled away. "This is no place to talk, Enoch. Meet me at the Criterion in an hour." She kissed him chastely on the cheek just as Lord Sedgwood and Alfie Barrington appeared behind her.

"Hello, Hale," Alfie said cheerfully.

Hale nodded. "Alfie. Your Lordship. Well, did you dig up any perfectly wizard old pharaohs?" He knew that they hadn't.

"Can't say that we did," Alfie admitted.

"The season has barely started," said the humorless Edward Bridgewater, fifth Earl of Sedgewood. "I'm sure that Carnarvon and his man Carter have hopes, but we have the better concession, eh, Alfie?"

The time Hale sat waiting for Sadie seemed almost as long as the three months she'd been in Egypt. In that three months, Sedgewood had been successful in his negotiations with the newly independent Egyptian government. He had sole rights for two years to a section of the Valley of Kings and second pick at the booty, if there was any. But tea and scones at the Criterion Restaurant wasn't exactly what Hale had in mind for his romantic reunion with Sadie. Hadn't Holmes and Watson first met at the bar here? Hale entertained himself with daydreams of taking his lady love someplace considerably less public.

"Hello, Enoch." She sat down beside him, interrupting his reverie. "I've missed you terribly."

They embraced.

"All I want to know," he began as they pulled apart.

"Shhh." She put a finger on his lips. "Let me talk first. I've changed, Enoch."

The next half hour passed in something of a haze for Enoch as she talked about how she'd gotten a new perspective on life in Egypt, surrounded by all that antiquity. After the War, the only thing anybody thought about was getting the most out of today because there might not be a tomorrow. Now she understood that one had to think about the future, but be shaped by the past. Tradition, family . . . that sort of thing mattered in a way that a silly young girl just doesn't understand.

"Sadie—"

"That's just it, Enoch. I'm not Sadie anymore. I'm Lady Sarah."

"I say, Hale." He jerked around at the sound of Alfie Barrington's annoyingly jaunty voice. Alfie stood about an inch taller than Sadie—Lady Sarah—with straw colored hair combed to the left. He was grinning like the fool that Hale had always assumed him to be. "Not fair to monopolize a chap's bride, what?"

Hale stared at the woman he loved.

"I'm sorry, Enoch." A tear appeared at the corner of her right eye. "Alfie and I were married on the ship."

Notes for the Curious

This is an *historical* novel, and as such blends facts and fancy. Except for the Diogenes Club, the Drones Club, and the offices of the fictional Central Press Syndicate, all of the locations are real and accurately described. The Drones Club was the creation of P.G. Wodehouse in his Jeeves stories. Some of the characters portrayed here have been historical, while the others existed only in the imaginations of the writers. For the curious, we present a few facts on the real-life people who were involved.

Winston Churchill: At the time of our little mystery, Winston Churchill was about to be unemployed, though not out of work. He would lose his seat in Parliament but was busy campaigning for another, which he would gain in 1924. From 1924 until 1929 he was Chancellor of the Exchequer. He was against Home Rule for India just as he had been against it for Ireland. In the 1930s his political career was rather unstable as he pushed for rearmament in the face of a growing German threat. In 1939 he was again First Lord of the Admiralty, a post he had held and lost during the First World War. He became Prime Minister in 1940 and you all know the rest.

T.S. Eliot: Thomas Stearns Eliot was born in 1888 in St. Louis, Missouri. Biographers record that Eliot had a relationship with Emily Hale that began in his Harvard years. He would become a publisher, playwright, and a social and literary critic. In 1914, he immigrated to England and in 1927 became a British subject. His friend Ezra Pound, another expatriate, was instrumental in having Eliot's classic poem, "The Love Song of J. Alfred Prufrock," published in 1915. Eliot was one of the great poets of the twentieth century, awarded the Nobel Prize in Literature in 1948. But like most artists, his art did not bring wealth as well as fame, so he worked as a schoolteacher, a banker, and an editor. He died in London in 1965.

Dorothy L. Sayers: Dorothy was an only child, born 13 June 1893. She was best known for her mystery writing. However, she was also an accomplished poet, translator, and playwright, as well as a Christian humanist. Her ties to Oxford were strong, even having been born there when her father was a chaplain at Christ Church. Her first published work was a book of poetry in 1916 and her first real success was *Whose Body?*, a mystery staring Lord Peter Wimsey. (She claimed to have based him on a combination of Fred Astaire and Bertie Wooster.) At the time of our story, she worked as an advertising copywriter for S.H. Benson's advertising agency. Sayers and artist John Gilroy made Guinness Stout and Coleman's Mustard household words. Her personal life had a peculiar twist as she secretly gave birth to a son in 1924. The child was placed with her cousin Ivy and never recognized by Sayers until after her death. She married another author, Captain Oswald "Mac" Fleming, in 1926. She lived in Bloomsbury until her death in 1957.

Gilbert Keith Chesterton: Better known as G.K. Chesterton, he was born in London in 1874. Chesterton was a prolific writer, philosopher, Catholic theologian, and sometime artist. He wrote eighty books, about 200 short stories, 4,000 essays, and a number of plays. After an education at University College London, he worked for a London publishing house from 1896 until 1902. In 1901 he married Frances Blogg and they remained together for the rest of their lives. In 1902 he started writing a weekly opinion column for the *Daily News*. In 1905 he began writing for the *London Illustrated News* and continued with the publication for thirty years. Chesterton was considered quite a sight to see, standing six feet four inches tall and weighing about three hundred pounds. He had curly hair and could usually be seen wearing his trademark cape and crumpled hat, carrying a swordstick while smoking a large cigar. Besides writing for his own paper, *G.K.'s Weekly*, he also wrote for the *Encyclopedia Britannica*. He is best remembered for his love of paradox, his words of practical wisdom, his creation of the Father Brown mysteries, and his defense of Catholicism (to which he converted in the year of our story). Pope Pius XI invested Chesterton as Knight Commander with Star of the Papal Order of St. Gregory the Great. Chesterton died in 1936.

Horatio Bottomley: One of the queerest characters of the early twentieth century! Born in London in 1860, he was orphaned at age four and raised in an orphanage until the age of eighteen. At twenty-five he was before the court for the first time, defending a publishing and printing company he owned in a bankruptcy action and explaining missing funds. This type of court action would be repeated over the years. He sold Australian gold mining stock, both real and imaginary, and British stocks of the same ilk. In 1888 he established the *Financial Times* as a way to promote his schemes. Twenty years later, he was charged with conspiracy to defraud. The prosecution failed because his corporate records were in such disorder that the jury could come to no conclusion. In 1906 he had established a patriotic journal, *John Bull*. During the Great War, he called for Germany to be wiped off the map of Europe. Bottomley became exceedingly influential and spoke at recruiting drives all over England, for which he made a considerable sum. In 1906 and in 1910 he was elected to Parliament (thrown out in 1912 for bankruptcy) and again in 1918. In 1922 he was convicted of fraudulent conversion of shareholders' funds in his "John Bull Victory Bond Club" scam. He was sentenced to seven years in prison. He died in poverty in 1933.

Polly the Parrot: Polly was delivered, not born. In 1886 a certain sailor owed some money to the owner of the Cheshire Cheese Pub. One day a cigar box was delivered and put on a shelf. As the employees were closing for the day, they heard a whimpering sound coming from the box and opened it. Inside was a red, black, and grey parrot that would be named Polly, a present from the sailor. Polly quickly became a fixture. A great mimic, she was known for her rather colorful language and imitating of customers. She greeted everyone, did tricks, and on Armistice Day 1918 imitated the popping of Champagne corks more than four hundred times, finally dropping off her perch from exhaustion. When she died in 1926, her obituary was carried in more than 200 papers and announced on the BBC. They say that as she passed she breathed her favorite word—Scotch!

Rev. John O'Connor: Born in 1870, O'Conner was a Roman Catholic parish priest in Bradford, Yorkshire. He was the basis of G.K. Chesterton's fictional detective, Father Brown. O'Connor was instrumental in Chesterton's conversion to Roman Catholicism in 1922. He also received the poet and painter David Jones into the Church in 1921, and was associated with Eric Gill and The Guild of St Joseph and St Dominic at Ditchling. Chesterton met Father O'Conner in 1904 while on a lecture tour in Yorkshire. He was much impressed that so quiet and unassuming a parish priest had such deep insight into the human condition. Chesterton thought of using such a character as a sleuth, someone whom people felt would be very unworldly yet "in fact knew more about crime than criminals." In 1937 Rev. O'Conner published his own book, *Father Brown on Chesterton*. The real Father Brown died in 1952.

Rudolph Valentino: Rodolfo Alfonso Raffaello Pierre Filibert Guglielmi de Valentina d'Antonguolla was born in Castellaneta, Italy, in 1895 and would live for only thirty-one years. Valentino arrived in New York for the first time two days before Christmas 1913. He had not done well in school, his father had died when Valentino was only eleven, and the boy had trouble adjusting and finding work. Like most immigrants, he took what jobs he could find, eventually becoming a taxi dancer at Maxim's. He then joined a traveling musical show that took him to the West Coast. He even had a small part in an Al Jolson production, *Robinson Crusoe Jr.* By 1919, he was doing bit parts in silent films. He quickly rose to stardom status when he played the lead in *The Four Horsemen of the Apocalypse* for Metro. Released in 1921, it was one of the first movies to make over a million dollars. It was *The Sheik* for Lasky-Famous Players Studios, however, that put Valentino in the hearts of all young women. The next four years were turbulent for the star: two marriages; fights over pay, directors and scripts with studios; and a personal strike against Famous Players which kept him out of the movies for a year. While the women loved Valentino, the men stayed away in droves. They felt he was effeminate. Valentino collapsed at the Hotel Ambassador in New York on 15 August 1926 and was found to have appendicitis and gastric ulcers. He died 23 August of peritonitis.

Kate Meyrick: Born in Kingstown (now Dun Laoghaire), Ireland, in 1875, Kate Nason married a doctor named Meyrick who would eventually run a hospital for shell-shocked patients from the Great War. Having been abandoned by her husband, she took their eight children and moved to London, where she became the proprietor and hostess of numerous illegal after-hours nightclubs. The most famous and longest lasting was The 43, so named for its address at 43 Gerrard Street, Soho. The 43 was the ultimate meeting spot of the late night London crowd, even though it was located in one of London's red light districts. Rarely raided, The 43 had the paid protection of some of the police in the district. Still, Kate would go to jail five times and in 1926 received a sentence of fifteen months. A hands-on manager, she kept a collection of dance hostesses who were schooled in what was legal and what was not. She also provided good jazz bands, and good pay to her employees. Kate was a true entrepreneur, admired by patrons and the public in general. She died in 1933.

Sherlock Holmes: It is generally agreed that he was born 6 January 1854. William S. Baring-Gould speculated that his education was rather broad in that his family frequently traveled the Continent and he was exposed to many customs and languages. Early in his formal education he found that he had an uncanny ability to use inductive and deductive reasoning to solve problems. He decided on a career as the world's first consulting detective. In January of 1881, Holmes was just beginning to make a name for himself. But it was his meeting with Dr. John H. Watson that month that would propel his career into the stuff of legends. In more than twenty years of active practice the team of Holmes and Watson changed the face of crime fighting. Holmes retired from the field at a still-young age and devoted himself to the keeping of bees and the occasional mystery that he could not resist. His obituary has never appeared in *The Times* of London.

A Word of Thanks

The authors would like to offer their special thanks for the support of the following people:

Ann Andriacco

Steve Emecz

Jeff Suess

Steve Winter

They also thank Arthur Conan Doyle for creating Sherlock Holmes, Dr. John H. Watson, Mycroft Holmes, Wiggins, Langdale Pike, and Shinwell Johnson.

About the Authors

Dan Andriacco has been reading mysteries since he discovered Sherlock Holmes at the age of nine, and writing them almost as long. His popular Sebastian McCabe—Jeff Cody series so far includes the books *No Police Like Holmes, Holmes Sweet Holmes, The 1895 Murder, The Disappearance of Mr. James Phillimore*, and (soon) *Rogues Gallery*.

A member of several scion societies of the Baker Street Irregulars since 1981, he is also the author of *Baker Street Beat: An Eclectic Collection of Sherlockian Scribblings.* Follow his blog at www.danandriacco.com, his tweets at *@DanAndriacco*, and his Facebook Fan Page at www.facebook.com/DanAndriaccoMysteries.

Dr. Dan and his wife, Ann, have three grown children and five grandchildren. They live in Cincinnati, Ohio.

Kieran McMullen discovered Holmes and Watson at an early age. His father, a university English professor, found his reading skills lacking and so, the summer of his eighth year, assigned him the task of reading the complete Doyle stories before school started again in September.

After a twenty-two-year career in the U.S. Army, twelve years in law enforcement, and twenty years as a volunteer fireman, Kieran turned to writing about his favorite literary characters, Holmes and Watson. His first book, *Watson's Afghan Adventure*, centers on Watson's war experience before he met Holmes. His subsequent novels, *Sherlock Holmes and the Mystery of the Boer Wagon* and *Sherlock Holmes and the Irish Rebels*, concentrate on the duo's wartime experiences. *Sherlock Holmes and the Black Widower* goes in a different and surprising direction.

Kieran lives north of Darien, Georgia, on a few acres with his Irish Wolfhounds and Percheron draft horses. He has three children and six grandchildren.

Also From Dan Andriacco and Kieran McMullen

London, 1920: Boston-bred Enoch Hale, working as a reporter for the Central Press Syndicate, arrives on the scene shortly after a music hall escape artist is found hanging from the ceiling in his dressing room. What at first appears to be a suicide turns out to be murder . . .

Also from Kieran McMullen

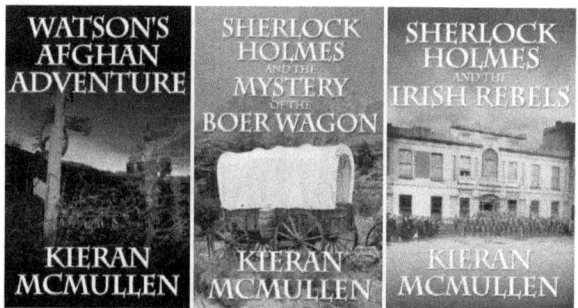

Three historical thrillers from the world's leading Sherlock
Holmes military writer.

"Exciting, and full of authentic military detail"

The Sherlock Holmes Society of London.

Also from Dan Andriacco

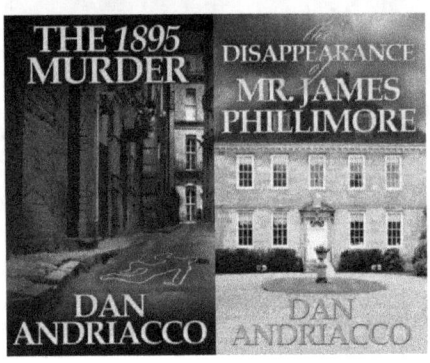

"*No Police Like Holmes* is an exciting and witty romp - not about Holmes but about his fans. The world's third-largest private collection of Sherlockiana has been donated to St Benignus, a small college in a small town in Ohio, and to celebrate, the college is hosting the Investigating Arthur Conan Doyle and Sherlock Holmes Colloquium."

The Sherlock Holmes Society of London

Four books so far in the McCabe and Cody series.

Also from Dan Andriacco groundbreaking
short story e-books

5 star reviews on Amazon Kindle

"Dan Andriacco has written a great Sherlock Holmes short
story; one of the pastiches I've ever read."

"The plot is complex for such a short piece but remains
very clean and concise, moving along rapidly to a surprising
conclusion."

Also from Kieran McMullen, one of the most controversial Sherlock Holmes stories ever written.....

Holmes has to investigate a potential serial killer who is accused of murdering his three wives. The name of the potential killer? Dr. John Watson.....

Also from MX Publishing

MX Publishing is the world's largest specialist Sherlock Holmes publisher, with over a hundred titles and fifty authors creating the latest in Sherlock Holmes fiction and non-fiction. From traditional short stories and novels to travel guides and quiz books, MX Publishing cater for all Holmes fans. The collection includes leading titles such as *Benedict Cumberbatch In Transition* and *The Norwood Author* the winner of the 2011 Howlett Award (Sherlock Holmes Book of the Year). MX Publishing also has one of the largest communities of Holmes fans on Facebook with regular contributions from dozens of authors.

www.facebook.com/BooksSherlockHolmes

www.mxpublishing.com

www.ingramcontent.com/pod-product-compliance
Lightning Source LLC
Chambersburg PA
CBHW051516170626
46811CB00002B/852